Foam World

Thor Spendel

FOAM WORLD

The moral right of the author has been asserted

ISBN 978-1-0686750-0-3

DEDICATION

To my wife for her support and encouragement (and putting up with my frequent staring into space).

CONTENTS

ACKNOWLEDGMENTS

Thank you to Julian Rathbone, author of "Nasty, Very", whose anti-hero helped inspire the idea underlying "Foam World". Thank you to Chris for unfailing technical support and helpful commentary.

1 JUNK START

Meeting

He took off the viewer, a pair of glasses with over-sized lenses to cover the whole field of view, and turned off the simfeed. He blinked a few times to adjust his vision and looked around; he liked to see what was really out there now and again, to 'feel the real' as they say. Minus the enhancement, the space before the junkyard gates was not inspiring. He rubbed the itch along the bridge of his nose - probably psychosomatic he surmised, given the viewer weighed almost nothing. There were two dozen or so people milling around in the space, though perhaps 'milling' was a bit strong - lounging, perhaps… he involuntarily looked up - a cloud crossing what could be seen of the sun, or a bird doing a rare fly-by; the sky was a sort of lowering yellow-grey, almost the colour of the storm clouds in Turner's stormy sea paintings, with the occasional thicker cloud looming through the murk. Nothing out of the ordinary, a bit duller than usual perhaps, though the air seemed fresh enough.

The walls surrounding the junkyard were white air-brick, though you wouldn't know it as the graffiti was so thick in places that the perfectly flat wall seemed to undulate. More interesting were the people, especially the other contestants, though he realised he shouldn't exclude himself seeing as he looked as daft as the rest of them. They were all covered in equipment, not just the super-light paraphernalia everyone wore but also weighed down with provisions for the coming ordeal - supposed 'contest'. More like gladiatorial combat it seemed to him, if more cerebral. He recognised the signs of those who never took real exercise, they always stood out because of their sheer awkwardness; it wasn't lack of muscle power, which was maintained in rigs automatically, but lack of use led to loss of coordination and balance, and left you bumbling about like an overgrown teenager.

It was hard to see peoples expressions beneath even the best lightweight gear - which still had to cover your eyes and mouth after all - but he tried to work out how the others were reacting using body language: mostly jittery, and on an adrenaline or other high, but he couldn't suss any obvious psychos, which was a relief - though appearances were not only deceptive but downright imaginary, so maybe he shouldn't assume too much too soon. Past contests had seen some memorable debacles: the one where a heavily trained samurai had simply overpowered the other contestants, one by one, trussing them like Christmas turkeys, then leaving them while he quietly went off to meditate on whatever he had in mind to build - except he didn't get the chance to complete his contemplation because the organisers had been forced by the threat of a hail of writs from family and friends of the other incapacitated players to summarily halt the contest, arresting the offending warrior with some difficulty and releasing the others; then again the one where a contestant built a large and very effective hand-held (if you were strong enough - he was) angle grinder-cum-chainsaw, which he promptly used to demolish all the other contestants contraptions, thus leaving his own - very modestly inventive - tool of destruction as the sole contender (he still lost, not original enough...); and, best of all perhaps, the one where a contestant heavily into neurotek built a neural disruptor which he used on the other contestants, making them walk around in a state of total confusion at the end of the contest. He actually won that one as the device, while not wholly original, was, at that time, an amazing piece of equipment to build from assorted junk (the rules were still changed, though, to prevent future wholesale demolition of contestants...).

He abruptly returned to the present as one of the others suddenly popped up in front of him:

'Ben, my man!'

'Hi Dec'

'So you're going for it at last!'

'Uh-huh'

'Well, don't overdo the enthusiasm'

'Sorry, Dec, it's been a long year, my stores of enthusiasm have been running low of late'

'Hey, I thought you were a leading exponent of the old nil carborundum movement!'

Benstan grinned despite himself, Declan never left you low if he could help it:

'You're right as always, Dec...'

'Course I am, course I am'

'...but this is still a heavy scene and I don't do collective inventions'

'Yeah, yeah, I know - hey, I don't *want* to share with anyone, not even my best inventor friend, I've already got a world beater in store!'

'You know that doesn't often work out, Dec'

'Just what is that supposed to mean, my man?'

'It means what you know it means - entering the contest with fixed ideas rarely produces winners, the whole idea, for Gods sake, is being flexible with what you find, the stuff changes all the time and trying to force it into preconceived ideas simply doesn't work'

'Who says so!?'

'I and all the judges say so - stop looking so surprised Dec, you know this game as well as I do'

'There's always the exception that proves the rule!'

'Like there's always a perpetual motion machine just waiting to be discovered around the corner, you *also* know that that stupid saying is just a misunderstanding about the meaning of "proof"'!'

'Well, maybe, and - then again - maybe not, you've got to admit there's always a bunch of basic stuff here - a *really* good idea that didn't need the more way-out junk could always be built'

'Like a better mouse-trap - come on, Dec, if you had one you'd have already patented it, or even better got it into production before anyone noticed so you had the early sales killing'

'Huh, you sure know how to pour cold water on a guy, Ben, how about some positive thinking?'

'Dec, positive thinking only works with things that have some sort of real-world content, if you apply it to hot air all you get is super-heated gas'

'Har, har, very funny, you'll soon see whether it's hot air, my friend'

'I'm sure I will, and I wish you all the luck, Dec, even if I don't share your approach'

'You too, my man, you too'

Entry

Declans usual carefree grin returned for a moment before they both slipped their gear back on, having detected a change in the mood around them; the world immediately reverted to a bright sunny day with the more than life-size presenter looming over them:

'OK everybody, it's rock and roll time! The world is waiting breathlessly to see what amazing stuff you can come up with this time around!!'

More likely waiting to see us fall on our arses or faces Benstan thought sourly.

'You all know the rules!'

Then, just in case they didn't, the rules lit up in the air above the gates:

NO COMPONENTS - ONLY TOOLS

NO INCAPACITATING OTHER CONTESTANTS

THE CONTEST LASTS UNTIL THERE ARE TWO UNCOMPLETED GIZMOS LEFT

THE BEST GIZMO WINS!

Not a long list, Benstan thought... there were a few missing rules in his opinion, like 'no incapacitating other contestants gizmos' and 'no stealing other contestants ideas', but the rules were made more for the convenience and interest of the organisers and viewers, rather than the contestants... the announcement was continuing but was the same old horseshit, interspersed with the odd piece of useful info, which Benstan relied on his PA to intercept and which was mostly for the benefit of viewers anyway.

They started to file slowly - very slowly - through the entrance, the speed due to the fairly thorough search the contenders were subjected to; despite the 'no components - only tools' rule there were certain tools it would be stupid to allow, like 3D printers and foam generators (though there was plenty of foam in the yard), which would enable you to build just about anything in less than no time, the idea being you were restricted to the materials and components in the yard being manipulated in fairly simple-minded ways. Every year someone managed to smuggle in tools and/or materials that contravened this, which viewers regarded as part of the fun, and if the resulting artifact was good enough sometimes the perpetrators got away with it. He idly wondered of Declan was trying something of the sort, it would be just like him.

Just before he got to the gate there was a scuffle and raised voices that he assumed was someone trying to hang on to an illicit item, though it didn't look like Declan; he switched his view to one of the floating overhead cams just above the gate. The unlucky or stupid contestant was gesticulating, red-faced with fury, at a blocky guard who was hanging on to something... he blew up the view - ah yes! - it looked like a gas holo-generator, a neat device that combined a 3D hologram with a light-sensitive gas which became entrained by the holo light and, once the projected form was full of the gas, a UV beam caused it to foam and stick together, converting the hologram into a solid structure which could be coated or filled to reinforce it - much faster than 3D printing and a much less bulky tool. But still obvious enough for these guys to find... Benstan guessed they were using one of the remote sensing teks to detect the foaming gas. Tough. A stupid idea anyway, you could hardly hide the use of such a large-scale constructor. Nanotech, now, that was much harder to spot, though the intense scrutiny they were all subject to, day and (night-visioned) night made even that hard to hide. He mentally shrugged, all such trickery was a waste of time unless the trickster came up with a genius world-beater, because the entertainment value of watching one of these semi-automated constructions was strictly limited - and entertainment was why they were here.

After what seemed half of forever it was his turn through the gate and he readied himself to stroll through, expecting no hassle. Wrong again. They tapped his main bag, he opened it, and they removed a very useful tool indeed, shaking their heads as they did so. What?! He didn't argue but didn't feel too pleased either... one of the guards pointed to a list glowing in the air above their heads, which included the device they'd just confiscated, a self-propelled pre-programmable foam reamer, very handy for converting large blocks of foam into useful forms. He rolled his eyes and sighed, the guard shook his head half sympathetically. Ah well. He walked on in, glad that only one tool had been confiscated at least.

He headed rapidly counter-clockwise into the 'yard'. which was actually a gigantic space for a junkyard, several square miles of all kinds of both mundane and esoteric remnants of centuries of tek, crowded like the basement of an enormous museum of artifacts both tiny and enormous and made from every material ever discovered or designed, from granite to buckyball syntactic plastic - even Benstan couldn't identify half of the stuff he strode rapidly past, despite his extensive knowledge of all things engineering. His strategy was to complete an initial survey, then separate himself from the rest of the contestants and keep it that way, with the help of intruder detectors - GNs usual intruder detection services weren't available in the yard, all net comms were cut for the duration. They still had their onboard facilities, a single person could easily carry computing power greater than that of the whole twentieth century, but it had been decided that dynamic access to the world net would make things just too easy.

It didn't faze Benstan, he couldn't see it made much difference given that you could locally generate whole virtual worlds, including high-powered SAIs like PAs. Still, it was inconvenient not to have facilities like auto intruder detection and it did waste some precious time setting up a local equivalent. Ah well, mustn't grumble. The second part of his strategy involved building a few semi-intelligent remotes to recce the immediate area for interesting devices and materials; he hadn't been bullshitting Declan when he said it didn't pay to start with preconceived ideas and he intended to produce a fairly full inventory of his surroundings before he got down to it - you often discovered amazing things amongst the junk which would give you a flying start in putting something interesting together.

Startup

He walked for the best part of the remainder of the day, a half dozen miles or so, before he set up camp, though building transport was an early priority so he'd be more mobile once he got properly started - he didn't intend to remain a sitting duck for too much longer, that would be asking for trouble. Still, first things first, he got out the self-erecting tent, a lovely phrase he always thought, and let it do its stuff while he put some water on the heater and retrieved some self-heating cans to replenish his energy reserves, he was pretty famished by now despite being more used to heavy exercise than most. After eating he felt almost human again and turned on his head night light, this was no time for sleep, tired or not he intended to work through the night constructing the various machines and devices he was going to need, there'd be time to sleep tomorrow when his intruder detection system was standing guard and no one could sneak up on him. He sounded paranoid even to himself, but in this game paranoia was a survival trait.

He'd stopped at a place full of relevant recent electronics whose functionality he knew well and the first task was an intensive dismantling and testing session to generate a good selection of working electronics of all sorts, processors, sensors and actuators, including a range of motors and housings. Power wasn't a problem, contestants were allowed a reasonable number of nuclear batteries and solar arrays were everywhere, efficient enough to overcome the murk, so come the morning there'd be power from the sky; he tested the assemblies by shining a daylight torch on them and checking the outputs. That done, several hours later he'd built several mobile searchers, essentially simple wheeled platforms with processors into which he'd downloaded state of the art SAIs pre-programmed to categorise the surrounding junk and hunt down especially useful or interesting stuff. He sent them off to do their thing and got to work on the intruder detection system - basically the same sort of thing but orientated to people.

All the while he'd been unobtrusively accumulating the materials to construct some mild anti-personnel devices - just in case... he couldn't be too obvious about it as, like all the contestants, he was under constant surveillance by media tek, which was entirely reasonable given the nature of the exercise, but he knew that since previous disasters, already mentioned, the media footage was minutely examined by SAIs programmed for dangerous devices, including weapons of all sorts, so he had to watch his step, as did the others. Nevertheless that wouldn't deter anyone determined to rip off other contestants in various sneaky ways and if any such came his way he'd be ready for them.

Unlike previous tek eras, where beginning with only raw materials could be a non-starter, the ability to build the tools to build the tools to build the tools was perfectly feasible when you had machine intelligence on your side, though it still required a little organisation and preparation; as he was both organised and well-prepared he started to build the most powerful tool of all as soon as his PA reported that the necessary parts had been located by his investigating remotes - a general-purpose fabrication robot powered by his own SAI software. The first version was a bit crude, but effective, and as the first thing it fabricated was a better version of itself, he was soon in charge of a full fabrication team, whose first official task was to create some transport, and first unofficial task to slyly fabricate the aforementioned anti-personnel weapons... these consisted of a low-power directional neural disruptor which would reduce anyone in its focus to absent-minded wanderings for an hour or two, and an SAI-controlled low frequency sound generator which could disable attackers in a variety of ways by modifying local conditions in various body parts, which might sound fairly innocuous until you appreciate that heating the blood in someone's heart by just a few degrees causes them to faint almost instantly... more dangerous than the neural disruptor though he instructed the SAI to only use 'safe' settings - it would be tough if someone threatening them with a projectile weapon turned out to be hyper-sensitive to infrasonics... Last but not least in this first phase he ensured that the second fabricator bot was supplied with additional software to act as a bodyguard if necessary. It was now mid-morning of the following day and he knew he wouldn't be able to stand up for much longer, so he ate the breakfast the first fabricator bot had cooked and fell into his sleeping bag...

Visitor

...to wake up almost straight away, or so it felt, except it was dark so he must have slept at least through the afternoon. His PA had woken him up, whispering quietly but urgently in his ear that an intruder had been detected and was being stood off by the second fabricator bot in its guard-dog role; his PA advised him to stay quiet until he'd fully woken up so he wouldn't be caught half asleep, good advice he immediately took, staying still and comming sub-vocally with his PA to suss the situation. The security remotes had detected the intruder while he was still a couple of hundred metres away, giving the fab bot time to park its current activities and reset to guard mode, after which it trundled off to meet the would-be intruder before he got too close. After the intruder had ignored the request to identify himself the bot had delayed him by the simple expedient of getting in his way and tripping him up, the bot was a metre high and weighed the best part of a hundred pounds so it was no pushover. The intruder tried to get hold of it but let go rather quickly when a medium low-power voltage was sent through its frame. Impasse - but by this time Benstan was wide awake and comming his minions. Even before he heard the familiar voice he'd guessed who it was, so he wasn't surprised:

'Hi Ben, what's with the heavy metal man?!'

Declan, of course. Even a normally trusting and easy-going individual would think twice about receiving visitors in this game - nobody, but nobody, paid social calls in the junkyard. So he didn't have a problem what to do, except he didn't want to show his hand weapons-wise this early if he could help it, though if Declan made any more determined efforts to get closer he'd regret it:

'What the fuck are you doing here Dec?!'

'Hey, that's not too friendly, as greetings go!'

'As greetings go, Dec, I can think of much less friendly ones, like bear traps, for instance'

'Jesus, what's with all the hostility and aggression?!'

'Don't come the dumb prawn with me Dec, you know as well as I do there are no allies in this game, that people - like you - are bribed in every contest to take out or rip off heavy-duty contestants, and the organisers don't fuss too much as long as life and limb aren't threatened'

'What are you accusing me of, Ben?!'

Benstan had already prepared the projectile screen and neural disruptor, so he wasn't in any real danger when Declan whipped out what looked like a taser and fired at him; the barbs were well-aimed but stuck harmlessly in the transparent and thin but very tough plastic screen between them, and the temporary 'security' bot instantly though invisibly fired a short disruptor burst at Declan.

'Just fuck off, Dec' Benstan finally replied in a low voice, more to himself than Declan, who was now standing blankly, the taser gun fallen nervelessly from his hand. The bot issued commands to turn around and walk back to where he came from - except going the wrong way, meaning he had three times the distance to cover going the long way around the junkyard perimeter. Once he started walking he would just keep going, unable to think coherently enough to countermand the instructions for several hours.

Benstan stood up and stretched, before sitting on the side of his new vehicle, now almost complete, to think about what had just happened. Obviously someone, or ones, among his competitors were serious about diminishing the competition by any available means, legal or not. Equally obviously his own fairly stringent security measures, which had seemed pretty extreme even to his suspicious mind, far from being over the top had, in fact, only just been sufficient. The critical question now was how much further they were prepared to go - if he spent too much time on security measures he'd probably fail to put the necessary time and energy into designing and implementing a world-beating gadget. Luckily he'd foreseen this scenario and had a contingency plan ready and waiting... he muttered coded instructions to his PA and sat down for breakfast, prepared by the first fab bot, now mostly relegated to domestic duties. It was time to review the wide-ranging analysis of materials and devices prepared by his investigative bots, and dream up his winning entry.

SUV

Two things stood out in the inventory: foams and controls. He had a very comprehensive range of foam types, from ultra-light filler/insulating foams to heavy duty (but heavier) high load and impact-resistant foams, including metal and ceramic foam composites which were considerably stronger than the strongest of the old steel alloys despite being less than a tenth their weight. For controls he had processors, sensors and actuators, including a vast array of every type of motor, coming out of his ears. He stood up and half-turned towards the vehicle the fabricator bots had constructed. Interesting. Now what if?.. he rapidly considered a series of replacements - make the wheels ten times bigger and a quarter the weight with high elasticity and containing light-weight ruggedised electric motors and you had a self-sprung four wheel drive with built-in redundancy, provided the rest of the vehicle was lightened likewise; make the seats with deep high-resilience memory foam and you more-or-less did away with the need for any heavy suspension. In fact if you made everything, including even high-strength load-bearing parts, from ultra-light foams... he quickly checked with his PA that this was feasible with what they had here - it was, just... then the whole vehicle would be extremely crash-resistant, bouncing rather than crumpling and breaking.

But that could be hazardous to the occupants, he realised the design would have to include automatic compensation for movement of the bodies being carried. No big deal, a combination of carefully positioned elastic foam, dynamic constraints and real-time motion control could hack it. Did he have enough processing power around though, not so much on-board controllers, there were plenty of those, but the high-power sims he'd need to resolve the dynamic design issues posed by the vehicle he was already building in his minds eye? Well, he hadn't skimped on software, if necessary he'd build new processor arrays from the stuff in the yard; he mentally rolled his sleeves up and got to work.

While Benstan was busy thinking his bot helpers were busy building a new bot, part of the aforementioned security plan, whose sole responsibility would be to create and run a secure next phase. As soon as they were done the humanoid security bot immediately started organising a move to a more secure camp, mainly to take them further away from the main route through the yard and build a ring-fenced zone that would be much harder for someone like Declan to get into; they couldn't move too far else the time spent building the resources directory would be largely lost - the clock was ticking - but distance was less important than sensible preparation of their new site, which would be just about impenetrable once completed despite there being almost no visible changes. A fair few artifacts lying around the perimeter of the new camp looked no different to before but were now rather different internally...

By the middle of the second night they were on their way, the new camp almost complete and the little army of fabrication, surveillance, guard, dismantler and mover bots significantly expanded. Benstan had already indicated the approximate areas of interest where he needed resources to be acquired and re-purposed and he was glad to get to bed for a good nights sleep - now on a proper bed and in the knowledge that any further attacks would be robustly repulsed and also that by morning he'd have the equivalent of a complete warehouse of appropriated materials and control electronics.

By late morning of the following day, after his first decent nights sleep in the yard, everything was ready. His PA casually mentioned over breakfast that several unofficial surveillance drones had visited during the night - their de-programmed components were now in storage; Benstan grunted acknowledgment before issuing instructions for the new venture, which would start with a materials testing programme and the building of a supersim orientated towards electro-mechanical testing. He was going to start with a general design sim, to get the initial body design sorted, and the next major task for the fabricator bots was to build a crash testing rig nearby - he left the details of extending the camps security perimeter to his PA and the security bot. Everyone got to work and he settled down to think about the look and feel of his new creation.

It was going to be big, no doubt about it, at least four cubic metres of body and wheel foam alone. He pondered the implications, would people accept such a big vehicle, and what about wind resistance? Tricky. He decided it shouldn't be too wide, certainly no more than the average truck bed, and reasonably streamlined... a tallish order but not impossible. Power-wise he was determined to make it a world beater, using a high-redundancy multi-compartment battery - in fact redundancy was going to be a major feature, he wanted to be able to drive this thing anywhere with the confidence that it wouldn't stop until just about everything had been broken off or worn out - both of which would be hard to do. This was going to be the ultimate anti-obsolescence drive, like some of the tougher mid twentieth century vehicles only a whole lot better. The upper body would be coated with high efficiency solar cells to recharge the light-weight plastic batteries powering the individual wheels and electronics - all of which would be super-low-power stuff. Hmm... this was beginning to sound expensive, he'd have to watch that, though there was a long tradition that the first of almost any new things started off as rich men's toys, so no change there.

H&S

The really tricky bit was going to be safety, he wanted to build, if not a fool-proof vehicle (you can always find a big enough fool) at least one that was hard to crash and burn - or, more importantly, hard to damage its occupants. The cunning plan he needed was a way to protect those inside against both their own stupidity and that of others in the vicinity, a taller order than mere electro-mechanics. The key was integrated and flexible systems that responded to every nuance and blip of the internal and external environments, including peoples behaviours... now where was he going to get them from?..

The answer was beavering away all around him, of course, the SAI bots... all he had to do was build the SUV as an SAI bot. 'All'... he knew well that this would be no easy task - SAI-inhabited vehicles hadn't been successfully made yet because there were known problems doing them; not only was it hard to control vehicles with the precision necessary to drive safely, but drivers hated not being in control of their vehicles, at least the ones they paid for themselves. This had always been the stumbling block for schemes to make driving safer by putting reliable and fast-reflexed machinery in charge, and Benstan knew it. He was going to have to think *very* carefully about this one... a concept developed in the twentieth century came to mind, just-in-time manufacturing, where you only hold enough components in stock to fulfill immediate manufacturing needs, saving the cost of warehousing huge quantities of stock... how about just-in-time accident avoidance and/or damage limitation?.. i.e. let the driver do his utmost to kill himself and any passengers but subtly (or not so subtly if necessary...) adjust the controls to prevent mad / drunk / reckless / stupid / high / inexperienced drivers from actually hitting things - or at least hitting them too hard. So, for most drivers most of the time, they'd be going where and how their own control settings dictated, but every now and then the SAI would trim the controls to prevent preventable accidents. The balance between sensible collision avoidance and irritating nannying would be hard to get right, but it was worth a go.

He was going to need even more sim power than he'd first thought, but for the purposes of the competition he was sure he could manage with what he had - provided his very visible machinery wasn't too easy to copy... he'd have a chat with the security bot about that... in theory you were allowed to keep secrets from the other contestants but not from the viewing public, who were, after all, paying for it all. Contestants weren't allowed access to GN and so couldn't see one another in the media feeds from the yard - but it was just too easy to get a line on GN transmissions for this to really be secure. So he'd have to be a little more duplicitous than usual... he discussed the problem with the bot, who suggested a simple ruse that would shield the more sensitive stuff, namely the SAI controls: do all the testing with a bot in the driving seat, while actually letting the vehicle SAI do the driving. Neat.

He soon realised the main test sim would need a lot more power than he'd brought into the yard, but there were loads of processors around surplus to the actual vehicle requirements and he always carried the software needed to configure supercomputer arrays from disparate individual processors, so he got to work constructing the enormously powerful array processor needed for the vehicle SAI sim: a 2.5D multi-vehicle environment - the N-body problem in real-time...

He'd discussed the vehicles SAI personality with the bots and they agreed that no existing SAI had exactly the mental structure needed, in particular the sneaky nature of the vehicle SAI, which had to exert control without seeming to most of the time while deliberately refraining from communicating with the driver, which was contrary to most current SAI designs - and if he didn't get it right he'd not only have a sneaky SAI but probably a psychotic one to boot, not quite the desired outcome. Luckily there were existing designs with similar requirements, such as SAIs operating in remote environments or surveillance ones, so he had the basics. He set up the supersim, loaded the vehicle characteristics and got to work on the psychology of a reticent control freak...

The key to the construction of the superdodgem - he liked the ring of the old-fashioned name, though the marketing people would change it soon enough - was a bunch of foams with two major characteristics: they were mildly elastic and they were light, enabling the vehicle to float and bounce rather then hurtle along like a landbound guided missile, which most previous vehicles were in reality. Being very light made for low fuel consumption and all-terrain use, including water, and being bouncy rather than crunchy made it very damage-resistant and, with the appropriate restraints, very safe. But therein also lay a serious potential weakness; a car that rattled its occupants around like castanets not only wouldn't sell, you wouldn't *want* it to sell, the cost of subsequent litigation from armies of whiplashed and otherwise injured owners would bankrupt you in no time. Contrariwise, being trussed up like grand prix drivers would look plain silly - hardly a macho image for an off-road SUV rider. He would have to use another softly, softly approach, where a cunning combination of passive and dynamic suspension and constraints made for a safe, well-protected ride without being too obvious. The cornerstone of the suspension would of course be the foam, a layer surfacing the cabin interior to damp external shocks, smoothing out all but the heaviest bumps, these requiring a more active suspension of foam blocks in which the wheel half-axles were embedded whose stiffness could be electrically adjusted in milliseconds; this lost a small amount of energy and traction but, combined with the 'floating' cabin, meant that actual restraints could be light and inconspicuous and only needed in extreme conditions of terrain and/or speed.

The combo of movement control by a high-powered SAI continually assessing both the drivers use of the controls and external conditions, and comprehensive but equally unobtrusive suspension, would make the superdodgem an exciting yet safe ride without overly nannying its occupants - a world-beater in personal transport if ever he saw one.

It took two days to build and test the array processor, by which time the basic design was clear in his mind, and the gathering and testing of materials and control units for both the vehicle and test rig was well advanced. The security bot had done its job thoroughly, not to say exhaustively, and nothing bigger than a bacterium could get through their defences without their knowledge; they were now as well-protected in their little kingdom as they would ever be and if Declan returned he wouldn't even get to within shouting distance. They were ready to rock and roll and they did: the fab bots were building sub-assemblies and test rigs to check out frame, drive motors and suspension components, as well as constructing a couple more of themselves, while Benstan concentrated on the new supersim with the help of his PA. Integrating the vehicle with a new SAI design was never going to be easy, even with the new superarray; they'd need to try out thousands of modifications to existing designs and test the effectiveness and stability of the resulting hybrids extremely rigorously if they were to avoid the disastrous consequences of a rogue SAI literally running away with its vehicle and occupants... this required speeded up time testing, the major reason for building the superarray in the first place, as it ate resources compressing years of testing into days.

Query

Within this short time the immediate area had been transformed into something resembling a full-scale manufacturing complex, so Benstan wasn't surprised when the special hot link that all contestants were provided with chimed:

'Hello, Mister Oakstaff?'

'Hi'

'Um... you seem to have rather a lot going on there'

'Yes'

'Would you mind explaining a little of what you're doing - we've received complaints from other contestants that you're monopolising rather a large part of the yard'

Surprise, surprise, the others bleating when they couldn't get their surveillance drones past his defenses. Benstan sighed:

'I needed to establish a manufacturing complex to build my new invention'

'And what might that be?'

They knew perfectly well that Benstan had the right to refuse to answer the question - no contestant was required to reveal his work until the end of the competition - but he guessed that the organisers were under pressure from powerful friends of the other contestants to find out what he was up to and it was too easy for them to dream up some new rule or regulation that would make his life difficult, even if the viewing public protested at the unfairness later, so he improvised:

'An all-terrain vehicle'

'Surely there's no shortage of those?'

'There aren't any like this'

The interrogator hesitated, he couldn't make it too blatantly obvious he was under orders from the other contestants, else they'd be instantly swamped by enraged viewers; Benstan just waited and let him sweat it out - if there was to be a battle of wills this guy had already lost...

'Um... OK, I suppose it's up to you to show that your creation is original'

'Yes'

The interrogator realised he wasn't going to get any further and he couldn't prove that Mr Oakstaff was doing anything wrong, so the others would just have to hope that their opponent wasn't as brilliant as they feared:

'OK - sorry to have bothered you'

'No probs'

The video cleared and Benstan grinned, he wasn't bothered in the least, and now that they'd shot their bolt there wasn't a hell of a lot else they could do short of wading in with guns blazing, which would instantly disqualify them no matter how well connected they were. He got back to FW, the Foam World supersim, and the emerging vehicular SAI, a fascinating character far more subtle than the game organisers...

SAIs...

The trouble with embodied SAIs is their tendency to wander off, unless they're completely moronic - which rather defeats the object. The distinction between an SAI which would override a dangerous manoeuvre and one which would simply override the driver for its own purposes - say to attend a driving event it had learnt of from GN - was rather finer than Benstan felt comfortable with, and took rather more to achieve than adding a few simple rules like the ones envisaged by Asimov. In the end Benstan had to regretfully compromise between the self-learning capabilities of SAIs based on massive processing power, which led to the very useful trait of self-preservation (and hence also preservation of the vehicles other occupants), but which also tended to develop into more self-willed behaviour, which would be unacceptable in almost any form in a driven vehicle; and the more automaton-like and simpler rule-based agents that were less flexible but more predictable. The high-powered SAIs he'd started with were more fun but altogether too dangerous, so he had to make do with a superagent instead, which could be set to only intervene when conditions were becoming dangerous and would be happily quiescent otherwise. The sim showed it to be a stable solution and by having other agents attend to more mundane aspects like the internal environmental control and load / power optimisation he could ensure the main agent kept its eye on the ball enough to reduce the chances of its missing anything important to acceptable levels. His low-profile nanny was complete, so he turned his attention to other matters.

One problem was finding or generating enough of the high-performance foams he needed - he'd already been warned by the bots that there wasn't time to build an entire chemical plant, as well as the engineering lab he'd already constructed, so they had to make do with what they could find plus a few neat tricks like restructuring existing foam with a judicious mix of radiation (heat, UV, microwave, whatever) and high-pressure treatment with chemicals they could formulate or cannibalise from the yard. He'd now been there the best part of a week and couldn't count on more than another (not that he'd want to, a diet now reduced to reconstituted dry food and vitamins was pretty uninspiring) - if he was caught out with an incomplete invention everything would depend on the reaction of the viewers to what there was, something Benstan rather doubted was the most reliable sort of judging... at least the bulk of the FW sim testing was complete, it was now mostly down to fabrication and field testing, though that included some pretty heavy-duty stuff, including the overall suspension balance and the multi-stage power system. This last consisted of both a solar power collection system fed from the upper body solar cells and a high-efficiency miniaturised Stirling motor / generator running on methanol, both of which charged a bank of light-weight plastic/lithium foam batteries. Just to cap it all, everything had to be waterproofed as the vehicle was to be amphibious, so all sorts of long-life seals and sealants had to be found or made.

Once they'd completed basic components like the body frame and the over-sized wheels, already well advanced, they could start physical as well as sim testing; he now had a dozen assorted full-size bots, as well as a couple dozen more small ones like the surveillance drones and materials scavengers, and his camp, or, rather, construction site, looked more like a busy factory floor than the temporary abode of a lone inventor. He knew his site would be one of the most heavily viewed in the yard, which made him practically immune from any further interference; even so, he wasn't taking any chances and the security bot was as busy as ever ensuring that their ring fencing of the site was difficult if not impossible to breach without their knowledge... still, Benstan wouldn't rest easy til the organisers announced that the competition was closed, at which point he hoped to drive in triumph to the evaluation arena at the centre of the yard. With his arms folded... something he hoped would make his opponents hearts sink as they realised what they'd missed in their undoubtedly exhaustive analysis of his operation.

Completing

The difficulty, of course, was that he couldn't *test* the vehicle with his arms folded, he had to appear always in charge, so he had to hope the sim tests were enough to get at least the worst bugs out of the superagent control software. He fleetingly considered a sneaky disconnection of the physical controls, all vehicles were now fly-by-wire so it wasn't hard to do a software disconnect, but he only had to do one action out of place and the ever-watchful SAIs he was certain were perusing his every move would instantly see that something was not as it appeared, so he would have to trust the sims for now, leaving final physical testing until after the competition and hope he didn't run over any of the judges...

By halfway through the second week he knew it would be only too obvious to his opponents what he was doing - hopefully excluding the superagent drive software - and they'd be spending as much time dreaming up reasons to disqualify him as completing their own gizmos; he was counting on their assuming his main weakness was originality, after all there'd been light-weight vehicles and amphibious ones and flying ones for a long time, so if all he had was a light-weight long-range amphibious job they'd be right - it was only the combo of this (admittedly pretty extreme version) with an intelligent controller that protected the vehicle and its occupants against almost anything that made it different from the story so far, hence the importance of ensuring no-one realised what he was up to.

It was now a race against time, he still needed a couple of days testing to be sure everything worked smoothly, so if everyone else was finished he was stuffed, all he could do was cross fingers and hope - apart from working 24 hours a day, of course, which he'd expected at the end of the show anyway. After another day they'd completed dry testing of all the main components, including all the controls testing it was possible to do without giving the game away, so he allowed himself to relax a little; the idea was that for the final tests the bots would enlarge and line a depression fairly close to the camp and fill it with water for the amphibious stuff, but he didn't get the chance, time had run out and the call came:

'Please instruct all your bots to down tools and make your way to the central test area within one hour'

There was no point diddling around now, it would take easily half that time just to get everything organised with all the bots (now switched to guard duties, not that he expected trouble this late on with the eyes of the world on everyone, but no harm being cautious...). The team he'd put together he intended to keep that way, they were a valuable asset and worth their weight in gold in the weeks and months ahead when he was completing testing and gearing up for full-scale manufacturing - he was that confident it was a winner, irrespective of the competition outcome.

Showtime

Their little armada set off, the humanoid bots in the two temporary vehicles flanking the experimental one and the remainder following up behind; it was no great distance to the centre, though negotiating the junk with their convoy slowed them down. As soon as he was in sight of the judges podium he took his hands off the wheel (the superagent had been driving anyway) and sat back, folding his arms - he knew all eyes were on him and no-one would miss the significance of his actions. The other contestants watched his approach with mixed reactions, some looking gloomy and others smiling ruefully even though they knew it probably signaled the end of their chances for this year. Declan wasn't present. Benstan wasn't surprised, he'd guessed that Declans only function was to breach his defences, as a 'friend', and incapacitate Benstan in some way. Declan just wasn't reliable enough to pass as a friend, he mused, they should have chosen their Trojan horse more carefully.

He belatedly emerged from his reverie as the judge repeated his question:

'Declare your new machine to the world!'

It was all for show, of course, which was fair enough. He'd applied a lot of careful thought to his reply - the balance between revealing too much at the outset and satisfying the viewers with a juicy soundbite was a fine one: if he made it clear that his vehicle was totally under software control it would put a lot of early adopters off, whereas if he didn't say anything about the driver agent he hardly had an original invention at all (though he reckoned the design and build quality alone would sell it):

'Welcome to the long-range all-terrain amphibious rover explorer - you can drive it anywhere, anyhow, in any conditions, and you'll have a damned hard job to crash it or even run out of fuel!'

'Is it SAI-controlled?'

Bloody hell, that was fast! Luckily he'd taken no chances and had an answer already prepared:

'No - just a little help from your friend when the going gets tough'

The sceptical look on the mans face showed what he thought of that, but he made no further comment - he knew outright opposition from a so-called 'judge' would only rally public opinion behind Benstan:

'Please demo your invention' he finished flatly.

This was a little tricky, apart from the lack of space to manoeuvre in there was no nearby body of water to show off the vehicles amphibious capability, but Benstan was confident that a little spectacular bad driving would capture the publics imagination, so he set to.

For this, of course, he needed to be hands-on, so he grabbed the wheel, aimed straight at the podium, and put his foot down. The startled looks on the judges faces was a joy to behold, he knew the video he was shooting as he drove (just a copy from one of the vehicles sensors) would be a sure seller later. To the judges evident relief the vehicle stopped dead six inches from the podium; Benstan grinned, threw it into reverse (even though he knew that in practice it would mainly operate in auto shift, for this demo a more spectacular manual style was needed) and roared back (sound effects, remember...) towards the other contestants, who did an equally petrified double-take as the vehicle stopped inches away from them. Having sufficiently amused himself at the expense of the others (though he also knew how much it would be appreciated by the viewers) Benstan drove rapidly at a nearby mound of debris and this time it auto-shifted into a lower gear rather than just stopping and easily traversed a bouncy path up to the top of the small mountain of junk, adjusting power and controls with lightning speed and precision as the debris shifted under the vehicles wheels. It wouldn't be apparent to spectators how much was being done by Benstan and how much by the driving agent - but what was very clear, more importantly, was that Benstan was having a lot of fun...

For the finale he deliberately drove too fast back down, choosing an unstable section he'd noted on the way up and, as he'd predicted, even the agent couldn't handle it and the vehicle tipped over forward and landed on the roof with an impressive crash - and bounced... Benstan swiftly released his belt and swung out from his upside-down position, with everyone watching agog, and pushed the vehicle with apparently superhuman strength onto its side and on over to right it, then leaped back in, gunned the drive (those sound effects again) and drove at speed back to the podium, to general cheering and somewhat less apprehension on the judges faces this time. There was no doubt about it, no-one was going to match this display, and if the judges attempted to disqualify or disparage his efforts in any way they'd be dog meat by the time the viewers were through with them. It was an undisputed triumph, he'd won and he and everyone else present (including a billion or so viewers) knew it.

2 FLOAT ON

Holiday

Winning the Junkyard Challenge was great fun and, in due course, very profitable - at least for my backers... Getting the superdodgem to production quality took a lot longer than I'd thought (or, perhaps, hoped), though transitioning from protos to production models always does, but once we'd developed the (fireproof!) superfoams and ironed the last quirks out of the superagent so that its actual performance more-or-less matched our marketing hype I felt I needed a holiday, and my long-suffering long-term partner, Eva, who had displayed the patience of an angel over the couple of years (years! I couldn't believe it and still can't) it took to complete the production model, felt - rightly - that she deserved a little attention too... so I embarked on what I hoped was to be an extended relaxing holiday with her in an experimental floating township on the Netherlands coast near Amsterdam.

My first impressions were rather mixed, I liked the idea of floating towns / cities but my engineering eye detected several of what I felt were unnecessary weaknesses, both in design and construction... but I determinedly clamped down on this reaction and resolved to just chill out and enjoy the ambiance and *not* start redesigning the place before I'd even settled in... and Eva knew me well enough to head off that sort of reaction anyway, and the welcome she and her friends prepared for me soon pushed the niggles back out of my mind as I settled down for some serious R & R. Living on water doesn't suit everyone, but it did me despite my total lack of sailing or even mild water sports experience - though I *could* swim, which I felt really ought to be mandatory for anyone whose activities took them near water (I was gob-smacked when Eva informed me quite seriously that it wasn't unusual in the past for sailors to be unable to swim). So, in a floating township, boats and a variety of water-sport-type artifacts (surf / paddle boards, water balls / wheels etc.) were very much in evidence and huge fun.

I resolutely resisted siren calls from my business associates to re-engage with the expanding market of uncrashable transport, but I couldn't resist quietly (surreptitiously, even, i.e. Eva would have thrown a severe wobbly otherwise) developing some designs that improved on the water toys we were playing with daily, using the palette of superfoams I was now so familiar with. Eva undoubtedly spotted the abstracted looks that came over me from time to time, but sensibly and determinedly ignored them and insisted we continue with the R & R. This went on for some weeks, until the day and night of the storm...

Storm

We were warned... the previous days weather forecast was, shall we say, ominous. I openly wondered how well this conurbation would withstand heavy storm conditions but Eva was adamant that they were up to the job so I shrugged and waited... the cloud bank that rolled in during the late morning was impressive (or terrifying, depending on your point of view...) and the gradual but persistent rise in wind speed during the afternoon put a stop to any water-based activities so, come early evening, by which time it was already as dark as a moonless night, we were reduced to settling by the picture window, the house already rocking steadily as bigger and bigger waves hit it, driven by the rising wind. Very soon after this the storm stopped merely toying with us and started in earnest.

Despite the so-called stabilisers that the floating houses were fitted with we were soon rocking and rolling until we had to relocate or tie down loose objects, including the furniture, if we weren't to feature in our own poltergeist action movie, and by now even just standing up was getting difficult. I decided that even though we had no chance of escape (outside winds were now over 100 kph) we should at least try to establish some sort of refuge where, if *anything* of this structure was to survive intact, we might stay more-or-less in one piece... the room we'd started in with the picture window was definitely not it, though we needed space for four people as two friends of Eva had joined us early in the afternoon and I'd persuaded them not to attempt to get back to their own place as I could see wind speeds were already too high to allow safe passage by the time they thought of leaving. The best place would be one with no external openings, windows or doors, and the only one of those was a short connecting corridor in the middle of the house.

By now we were having considerable difficulty staying on our feet, and getting the stuff out of the corridor - the obvious place earlier to stash the flying furniture etc. - was positively dangerous but had to be done, though we left anything soft like cushions and other soft furnishings, essential to at least reduce the damage of our whole bodies flying through the air if the oscillations of the structure got any wilder... eventually we got ourselves and enough soft stuff, including bedding I'd somehow managed to get down the stairs despite being thrown about like a roller-coaster rider, into the short stretch of corridor, with access doors sufficiently well jammed that furniture, appliances and, I suspected by now, bits of the building as well, wouldn't be joining us... even so, and clutching cushions and blankets and other soft furnishings to ourselves, we were still being thrown around enough to get well bruised, however hard we tried to wedge ourselves into corners or between the corridor walls.

At this point I was beginning to wonder, in the fractions of seconds I was able to think at all between watching / feeling out for the others (the lights had long gone), whether the entire house was about to be battered to pieces, including, obviously, our refuge - it was only a matter of time before that happened because it was clear to me from the shuddering / crashing / creaking noises that our little piece of corridor was about the only thing left more or less intact, albeit we weren't enjoying our safety overmuch... then the howling / shrieking of the wind, which I'd grown so accustomed to that I hardly noticed it any more, began to abate a little, and, gradually, the terrific rocking and rolling of the whole corridor abated to just heavy shaking, and the crashing and banging on the walls of various items - furniture, bits of doors and windows, whatever - stopped, and we could hear ourselves speak again and then, so suddenly it was like the abrupt ending of a dream, the storm was over. We gingerly picked ourselves up, becoming conscious as we did so of a whole new collection of bruises and pains that manifested themselves now that the attention grabber of a roller-coaster had ceased. If there had been any light we would doubtless have looked at one another disbelievingly, but I immediately checked that everyone was at least able to answer a simple question, albeit with a groan or two thrown in.

Aftermath

The corridor doors opened outwards , presumably because it was so cramped, and we found all of them barred by debris on the other side; once we'd organised ourselves and stopped accidentally kicking each other or poking each other in the eye in the dark, we decided on a concerted push against the door leading into the living room with the picture window, which seemed to have a little more give in it than the others. So we pushed, and pushed, and eventually the obstruction on the other side gave way - it was the remnants of the picture window... luckily (sensibly...) it was made from shatterproof plastic so at least we weren't contending with a field of broken glass... we stumbled out of the corridor and stared uncomprehendingly at the - now moonlit - scene of devastation before us, made all the clearer by not having a picture window in the way any more...

For a start, we were no longer amongst a little flotilla of other residences, what confronted us was mostly open sea with myriad pieces of floating wreckage and homely debris... we just stood there, struck speechless for a while, aches and pains temporarily forgotten, wondering... where was everybody? And, more to the point, where were *we*?.. either we'd been separated and blown a long way or were just very lucky to still be afloat... I desperately hoped it was the former, but had a horrible sinking feeling that it might be the latter... dragging my eyes away from the chaos I looked more closely at what was left of our own abode... not much... the short corridor had been an inspired choice, though there hardly seemed to be any other option to be honest. We hugged one another in wordless grief... then I got a grip and checked our current status, at least the storm hadn't disabled the net (though that was rather unlikely given the level of sat coverage); I couldn't contact any neighbors, though I realised that was hardly

surprising as they'd still be in survival mode even if OK... I
checked my superdodgem, it was still running despite a severe
battering and was on its way now it had a fix on our position - an
unusual version of the cavalry I grimly smiled to myself.

Requiem

The news wasn't as uniformly bad as our first impressions
indicated, but neither was it very cheering... the majority of our
small population had survived, largely by being elsewhere,
including those who lacked Evas' confidence and had decided
discretion was undoubtedly the better part of valour, but there were
several fatalities (and many more in the pet population), along with
a horrendous roll of injuries, some serious, and even though our
own consisted only of a selection of bruises and sprains we felt
pretty battered for some time. We attended several funerals and did
a lot of hospital visiting, while living in emergency
accommodation provided by coastal services, before leaving the
immediate area and setting up house on solid ground, at least for
now.

Ideas

So my original misgivings about the robustness and general design
sloppiness (as I saw it) of the floating burgh hadn't been so far off
the mark after all... time for a little rethink of floating living. It was
clear that the old assumptions about the frequency and severity of
storms in this part of the world ('nowhere near the power of a
typical tropical storm' ho ho) were due for a radical reassessment -
even if storms as bad as this were infrequent, you only needed *one*
of them to dismantle floating structures as currently designed... it

seemed obvious to me that you should be designing for the worst eventuality if it was where you were going to live for a long time... could I do better, I wondered? Of course I could!

One of the major problems with existing efforts to gild the sea with useful structures was the side-effects on marine life: unless you designed your structures and associated activities with immense care you tended to produce a noisome soup of poisonous waste instead of a wholesome sea surface. I realised that this wasn't something to be tackled as an afterthought, it needed to be designed out by considering the needs of marine life *before* putting things on the sea. A little careful thinking revealed a few simple principles that would help to achieve the desired outcome of healthy homes on a healthy sea, such as not covering more than half of the sea surface to allow light through for seaweed and other marine life; disallowing tall structures for the same reason, as well as storm safety (!..); preventing *any* pollution into the underlying water, meaning 100% strict waste management; encouraging marine organisms to grow on the underside of *all* structures - previously called fouling - enabling them to act as nurseries for fish and other denizens of the sea. That sort of thing, hardly rocket science, and yet frequently disregarded in practice.

Now I had to get down to actual structural design - what sort of things would work sensibly on something as unstable as a stormy sea? One of the things I'd noticed was how often 'artists impressions' of sea-living showed nice-looking houses bobbing gently on little wavelets in sunny conditions with blue skies - to my sceptical (and now experienced...) mind entirely the wrong picture to work to - a *much* better one is a beach house being shredded by a tropical storm, *that's* what you're dealing with on the sea, especially in these globally warmed days when vast tracts of coast have already been overwhelmed by a combo of fiercer storms and rising sea level. The only structures that have been proven to be resistant to such conditions using relatively ordinary building materials (i.e. not six-foot thick granite) are geodesics, Buckminster Fullers wonderful self-supporting spherical (or hemi-spherical) frames. I took these as my starting point for structures above the waves. Now for those beneath them, the platforms on which my structures would be floating, it was clear to me that the only practical platform was one that couldn't be sunk - in *any* conditions... something I called permanent buoyancy, and the only tek that made sense here was superfoam, lots and lots of it. I set to work.

I was immediately struck by what my initial quick and dirty visualisations of these stable structures looked like – bubbles... in fact rather similar to some of the less angular artists impressions of 'cities of the future' beloved of early sci-fi. Such roundness may have been largely unnecessary on land (unless you lived in tornado alley) but for survival on the high seas they were practically mandatory - at least as long as you weren't building reinforced concrete castles on the sea, which would obviously defeat the whole object of the exercise by boosting carbon dioxide in the atmosphere to even more eye-watering levels.

Once we had some proven prototypes we'd need to consider the mass production and marketing which, for me, would have been harder than the tek, except that in ramping up volume sales of the superdodgem I'd already had to wrestle with such problems so I had a number of inspired marketing people in mind, the sort who can sell fridges to the Inuit (though that's not so funny as it once was, with most of the Arctic melted) - but the difference here was that the unfortunates being dispossessed wholesale by deteriorating coasts were crying out for replacement accommodation, *and* they were used to living by the sea (and some, of course, actually on it). As usual there was a sizable delay while I used sims and protos to hammer the initial designs to find the (numerous) flaws, which gave the materials, fabrication and marketing people time to get their act together - here as everywhere preparation is half the job (unless you want to risk wholesale operation of Murphys Law).

Biorings

One of the more esoteric problems I found myself grappling with was persuading backers to part with funds for what I called 'protective aquaculture', or biorings, a very effective way to ameliorate the effect of waves and storms on floating structures by surrounding them with acres of seaweed or other marine or modified shore vegetation (such as floating mangroves), which acted like a more robust version of oil on water and had the additional advantage of boosting marine productivity and biodiversity (provided you placed the installations away from ecologically sensitive areas like corals or sea-grass beds). The trouble was it substantially increased the cost without boosting short-term revenue. I soon saw that I was only going to progress this by getting governments and marine organisations on my side, including putting their hands in their pockets for additional funds so private / corporate backers wouldn't be shouldering all the up-front cost and risk - not so unreasonable since in the medium term (a few years) the considerable boost to both food production and amenity would easily outstrip both setup and maintenance costs. By 'accidentally' revealing the increased risk of *not* providing these biotic buffers (a series of shots of my floating house after the storm...) I raised the profile of the issue sufficiently to get some additional investment, at the cost of a few black looks and grumbles from my sponsors... well, they shouldn't get their own way *all* the time.

We now had enough starter funds to sort out initial material development and detailed designs plus protos for some floating installations, starting with non-residential functions like power generation / desal / coastal stabilisation, for which we soon discovered there was no lack of demand, helped by some earlier failures in major storms (for which, admittedly, we had as yet only theoretical solutions). Once we had some successful protos it was clear we'd have a deluge of orders for our floating marvels, though it still proved difficult to prise the development funds for the associated defensive biorings out of our sponsors tight fists, but persistence and a little gentle arm twisting achieved a modest effort at ringing a couple of smallish protos with greenery and the difference in behaviour between them and previous efforts minus the greenery in a couple of mild(ish) storms was pretty convincing, though it did create a problem with beach invasion by our green ring in one proto... which provided useful experience in tackling the effects of movement of our complex structures due to driving wind...

...and highlighted a perennial problem with floating structures: we didn't want hard anchors to the sea floor because this created a high-resistance target for storms and waves generally to worry away at, yet moving such potentially complex structures back to where they belonged wasn't straightforward... we could slow movement down with a combo of low profile design, water anchors and attached marine growth, but tides and currents, as well as wind and storms, would eventually always move them, albeit slowly. What to do? One blessing of being on the sea was we weren't short of energy, there was plenty of solar / wind / wave energy to be had, the question was how to harness it. After various schemes had been floated (kites...) we hit on a crude but effective strategy of 'current reversal'; by attaching super-strong nets and hawsers to loosely hold the different parts of our floating collections together and then running high-power pumps that moved quantities of seawater from one side of them to the other, so producing a slow and stately progress in the direction of pump inputs - not particularly efficient but as the energy was free and we didn't need to run it all the time it would be good enough to prevent slow migration to unwanted destinations (like beaches). On the other hand, it might just be easier to have a few electric tugs around.

Production

It took us a couple of years to prove our ideas with protos, including the biorings (which also proved spectacularly successful at stimulating both marine productivity and biodiversity, provided we kept the light occlusion down), during which time we were going hell for leather at extending the range of superfoams suitable for sea conditions and sorting out the practicalities of services (like making electric power nets seawater proof...). We also did a lot of sim design in an updated FW, which catered for the peculiarities of structures built on a variable moving surface. And our marketing benefitted from the shitstorm of coastal damage which was still accelerating on coasts all over the world, despite the now relatively successful efforts at curbing carbon dioxide increase - unfortunately inertial effects apply equally to natures systems as human ones and the trillions of tonnes of water added to the seas from melting ice caps and glaciers would take a considerable time to put back again.

The net result was that our potential market grew to meet us, including a large residential requirement that in theory we hadn't even built the protos for... luckily FW had as much residential accommodation on display as you could want and even without the protos the accuracy of the supersim had proved itself on a number of issues already and repurposing existing fabrication from other - admittedly very similar - structures was the work of days rather than years. Floating conurbations (complete with biorings) flew from the sim screens to the factory floors to meet the burgeoning demand and almost in the blink of an eye we became the worlds largest manufacturers of floating prefabricated residential accommodation.

Of course there was still considerable resistance to the substantial extra cost of the biorings, but we were helped by experience with the other structures - which included geodesics - that we'd been putting on the sea for a couple of years, which conclusively demonstrated the superiority of structures complete with surrounding greenery - it might take longer and cost more but when the shit hit the fan with escalating winds and storms there was no doubt about the winner, ones with greenery survived and ones without didn't, so even the most so-called 'hard-headed' investors could clearly see the results of skimping on what they'd originally regarded as over-engineering... so they gulped and stumped up the extra funds and we had a new breed of garden city, compliments of the worsening weather. Over time, of course, as with most large-scale enterprise, it got cheaper as the meshes and nets and produce processing centres and marinas proliferated and the cadre of watery gardeners grew... eventually the economic output of the increased marine productivity alone paid for the extra herbage and I gave a sigh of relief that extending human colonisation to the sea hadn't simply added to our already ruinous impact on the land.

3 BLOOPS

Mars tek *[1] - tough times ahead...*

The first thing to remember when designing new teks for Mars is that practically nothing that works fine on Earth does on Mars. Mars conditions - from a machines point of view - are not good news. Mars is very cold, almost (but not quite) airless, with extremely variable surface conditions, high radiation (that lack of atmosphere) and, at a third Earth's gravity, nicely designed to cause most objects - including vehicular traffic - to not behave as expected. Oh, I almost forgot, it's also subject to extreme dust storms that - despite the thin atmosphere - are capable of scouring the surface of most artefacts in a surprisingly short time. Quite a challenge.

It isn't just that things have to be stronger / tougher / lower friction / harder etc. but that most 'ordinary' things have got to be completely rethought to work well in the Martian environment. Anything that's affected by highly penetrative and corrosive dust, or high UV radiation levels, or can't be easily relocated if lost / dropped / blown away, or has high energy requirements, or low on-board energy storage, or is difficult to use under difficult conditions, or is hard to maintain or repair (in other words, the sort of things we've routinely come to know and love on Earth...) is not Mars-compatible.

So... every Martian design is high-reliability, hard to break and easy to mend (and by ordinary if technically proficient people rather than brilliant specialists), self-monitoring, easily relocated when mislaid, auto-recharging (everything that can be is covered with high-efficiency solar cells), wear resistant and tolerant - and easy to use (because the people using it are subject to the same conditions as the equipment). No probs.

Fun

Floating hordes on the high seas was exciting for a while and my superdodgems were good fun, but, as always, I soon got bored and then restless... my sponsors were in a (for them...) good mood, which I knew from hard experience wouldn't last, so I started to look to the skies. I decided that if I could build floating cars and houses I could do just as well with flying ones... it was time to progress from floating to flying and it all started with my bloops, which were a sort of mongrel cross between airships and light aircraft, ending up with superlight and highly manoeuvrable aerial runabouts.

The key ingredient of the bloops, that started the whole bandwagon off, was the development of super-light and strong foams in the middle decades of the twenty-first century, versions of which I was already highly conversant with from my work on the superdodgem and floating sea structures. Foams you could make nearly unbreakable wings out of, yet pick up room-fulls with a finger, were obvious candidates to make lots of interesting and fun machines from. Cycles with foot-wide, six-foot diameter wheels, that you could ride anywhere, including over water. Solar-powered hovercraft that could be driven like dodgems in complete safety - for the external world as well as the occupants. Water-balls, gyroscopic pogoes, skate-logs... But getting to the next level - flying in 3D - and, more to the point, doing it safely, would require a lot more effort, starting with major expansion of my faithful sim world, FW.

Flight Sim

FW, incorporating the best of the safety sims, was a variety of supersim (supersims, put simply, are just sims that are so good you can't tell them from the real thing unless you specifically invoke special control features, like materialising stuff from the sim genie). I'd realised early on with the superdodgem that fun transport that let idiots kill themselves would have a limited appeal; not so much for the punters (most young men - and quite a few young women - believe themselves immortal until they're dead) but for the authorities, who accept the relatively low kill rate of expensive toys for the rich but would balk at the carnage that would ensue if the price of self-immolation dropped too low. I'd already developed for the superdodgem a nifty way of designing out the unfortunate consequences of the death wish that seems to grip every other driver of fun but potentially lethal vehicles. The standard safety sims were a great idea for testing the design and build of more mundane transport, which was loaded with warnings and crude fail-safes - but individuals bent on excitement weren't impressed with such nannying devices that turned the whole experience into a chore.

So Kevin and his team set about extending FW for flying vehicles to combine imaginative new ways of crashing into things in 3D with a high element of personal safety - a contradiction that nobody previously had got quite right (at least not in a way that was transferable - engineering wise - from the virtual to the real world). I started by minimising the consequences of crashing in the first place. Fliers who've experienced the effects of crashing into dense but reasonably soft undergrowth will appreciate that, provided your harness holds and the whole thing doesn't burst into flames (almost impossible with modern batteries and solid lubricants anyway), you can crunch up quite a lot of soft green stuff with reasonably thin supporting bits without doing yourself over-much damage. So we first of all created a subsim with almost total ground cover consisting of large but squishy plants.

From here we could build a sim safety control system that would be the successor to my superdodgem superagent, to create the illusion of daredevil piloting while actually keeping you as safe as sitting in the sim rig itself. The clever bit was it wasn't obvious. You got in, pressed Start, and you were in complete control - not. There would be short, medium and long-range sensors operating over a fair spread of the frequency spectrum, with various wavelengths impervious to various types of atmospheric conditions - rain, fog, cloud, dust, whatever - integrated with GN GPS (you *never* get lost, whatever you might think) and you *cannot*, however hard you try, crash in a way that would injure you, your passengers, your vehicle, or anything in your immediate vicinity more solid than the aforementioned squishy plants. But - and this is the important bit, as indicated above - it isn't obvious: you don't get loads of boring warnings, you *are* allowed to do hairy-looking things that, despite appearances, are within the vehicle's capability (and yours, of course; medical monitors constantly check your state of health and warn the control system to cool it if things get out of hand).

Mars tek *[2] - I'm a mole and I live in a hole...*

On Mars the safest place to be is under the ground (in a literal rather than metaphorical sense...). On Earth small animals often dig holes, larger ones either find (or steal) bigger holes - or stand in the rain and put up with it. Except for the ones that are clever and dexterous enough to build their own shelters, of course. Back to Mars:- there, it's sensible to combine the two approaches and build holes in the ground, preferably with sun-facing (UV-proof) windows on the surface.

Of course, like everything else Martian, a Martian hole is rather more than your average common-or-garden hole in the ground. The floor / roof / walls of your Martian hole must be leak-proof (gases as well as liquids), super-strong, and vibration damping - and made of readily-available local materials. So brick tunnels aren't going to do the job, or even, for that matter, standard high-strength lightweight concrete. The tek for formulating foams with a range of precisely specified characteristics had to be well advanced before the ideal Martian building material could be made. It has to be made from Martian rock and carbon dioxide, the only materials commonly available on Mars, as well as requiring minimal process energy and materials (e.g. tens of thousands of gallons of water, a la paper-making on Earth, is a no-no on Mars).

A tall order, perhaps, but by utilising modern fabrication methods such as substituting liquid carbon dioxide for water as a solvent / transport and harnessing bacteria to chew up Martian rock dust (with a little solar-grown bacterial feed added), new tek was developed to process Martian rock into super-strong building foam. Voila - Martian all-purpose bases, built to last.

Bloops!

By now FW, packaged as a superior flight sim, was itself making money hand over fist, it almost seemed unnecessary to graduate from the virtual to the real world, but both I and the sponsors knew that if we didn't do it someone else would, and they'd probably make a hash of it and generate more litigation than revenue - and the opportunity to make more money than Croesus would effectively have vanished (assuming, of course, that *my* designs worked as well with real-world physics as in the sims, which could never be guaranteed...). So, I gathered together a bunch of intrepid aviators / sports people / racing fanatics / lunatics, with assorted pilots licenses, and initiated the transfer of detailed designs to production facilities (which was almost fully automated, despite the newness of the tek - you just had to have the money). And watched as everything fell apart...

No big deal, I'd expected nothing less and wasn't unduly downcast (well, to be honest, I was pretty pissed - just not particularly surprised that there were still disagreements between the virtual and real worlds). The pilots took it good-humouredly enough, they were pretty well protected and used to rough handling anyway, plus we'd installed some last-ditch safeties in the protos to try to not get anyone actually killed... Good job, too, nearly all the pilots who did the first flights ended up crashing seriously and spectacularly into the ground, support buildings or each other - and being cushioned by air-bags or foam surrounds or balloon jackets, or whatever, is infinitely superior to direct, crunchy contact. But we got the safeties and their software sorted gradually, and firstly serious accidents dropped and then stopped, then the minors lessened, and when the pilots started complaining how flying this stuff was no fun any more we knew we had it licked.

That's when they started referring to the vehicles as 'bloops'. This gave us pause for thought - did we want what could easily be seen as a negative sort of handle to become common usage? In the fun vehicle market image isn't *quite* everything... In the end I pointed out to the investors that there wasn't a damn thing we could do about it, trying to 're-educate' hard-bitten pilots to use some other - presumed more flattering - terminology would simply be a waste of time, and, more importantly, would draw attention to our fears about its potentially negative marketing effect, immediately creating a self-fulfilling prophecy. Luckily I reacted in time and everyone continued talking of the 'bloops' in a laughing rather than a sneering way and the marketing people gently steered the publicity into a more positive tack on the name. We breathed a collective sigh of relief and handed over to the sales and distribution network people, whose enthusiasm for bloops soon became infectious and sales took off overnight.

Mars tek [3] - CHON delights...

Humans need CHON - no, not a newly discovered vitamin, but Carbon, Hydrogen, Oxygen and Nitrogen. Earth has loads of CHON, a massive abundance, most usefully in air and water. Mars... well, let's just say we have a little problem. Mars has pretty large quantities of carbon dioxide in its atmosphere, and has more, together with water, frozen at or near its poles. Nitrogen (like uncombined oxygen) is only present in the atmosphere in very small quantities, but more can be extracted from the rock (and building foam specifically doesn't include nitrogen in its composition).

Net result: getting CHON in reasonable quantities on Mars is hard work. Water-and-carbon-dioxide-ice is collected near the poles and additional carbon dioxide is extracted from what little atmosphere there is. Processing rock for CHON goes hand-in-hand with rock-foam manufacture. This is why the rock-foam has to be a good gas-seal, not only to stop the pressurised air leaking away and letting the inhabitants die of asphyxiation, but because it's so expensive to make breathable air in the first place.

So the efficiency of Martian CHON recycling isn't just average, or even good, its positively brilliant and constantly being improved. You waste CHON on Mars and sooner or later you kiss your ass goodbye...

Going Large

Time to grow up... airship tek had been developing for a long time, with a lull around the middle of the twentieth century but a massive surge at the beginning of the twenty-first when governments and corporations at last started to take the possibilities of future oil shortages and rampant global warming seriously (still too late, but there you go). You can cross the Atlantic on a tiny fraction of the oil needed by one of the old-style jumbo passenger jets if you give yourself a day, rather than a few hours, to do so. The virtual indestructibility of well-constructed bloops also boosted their popularity, especially when the costs of hardening conventional air transport against extreme events such as terrorist attacks and unexpected storms (much more frequent now) was factored in. So airships, in the guise of bigger versions of my bloops, made a comeback, with better designs that made them more stable and maneuverable than earlier models, as well as being demonstrably safer than any other form of transport, including walking. They soon had the edge on other types of air travel for any but the most extremely time-conscious.

This didn't happen overnight, of course. The original bloops, which we'd now been working on for years, were considerably smaller, but with the same tek: super-light-weight (some of them had negative weight, due to hydrogen or helium gas foaming, i.e. they floated in air) yet immensely strong materials; minimal energy consumption, using solar- and wind-energy converters combined with light-weight energy storage (some of the structural foams doubled up as energy storage devices); and intelligent sensors that almost gave them the responsiveness of birds rather than machines and enabled pilots to boldly (and, more to the point, safely) go where angels fear to tread.

Not that I got much out of it, mind you; by the time development and pre-production and production and marketing venture capital had been taken on board, my share was down to a fraction of a percent - though I had the sense to ensure it was on turnover and not profits (profits, of course, are an accounting fiction which can be manipulated to be almost anything - including nothing). I wasn't bothered, I was pretty sure there was more where that came from, and a small fraction of an awful lot can still be a sizable income, as anyone on the lucky receiving end of global GN micro-payments can testify. Anyway, I'd hardly started yet: the bloops, big and small, had been fun, but the more I worked with the materials and engineering the more possibilities suggested themselves...

4 ALOFT

***Mars tek** [4] - suit you, sir?...*

*'Clothes maketh the man'. This has always struck me as a daft
statement, perhaps because I generally go about like your average
well-dressed scarecrow. For sorties out on the surface of Mars,
though, it's got a lot going for it. Mars surface conditions are such
that you need to be very well dressed indeed. A Marsuit isn't quite
like a spacesuit - though you could use it in space at a pinch - but
it's got an equally high spec. One of the more stringent
requirements is the level of dust resistance; a Marsuit has to be
able to withstand several days at least in a Martian dust storm,
which can abrade and - even worse - penetrate the toughest of
Earth's all-weather clothing in short order, despite the thinness of
the atmosphere. But with such a low atmospheric pressure a
Marsuit has to have as good a gas seal as a spacesuit, and not
only to protect the occupant from low pressure but to conserve as
much as possible of the precious CHON - so you don't just vent
breathed air, at the very least you have to extract the water vapour
in it first (and the more advanced suits recycle the carbon dioxide*

51

as well by using solar power to combine it with the water vapour to produce oxygen and methanol).

So a Marsuit is quite a production, with its abrasion-resistant self-sealing outer skin, transparent to allow the solar cells beneath to augment the built-in power supply which is necessary to drive the full environmental conditioning unit, consisting of controls for temperature, moisture and oxygen, together with resources to meet a variety of situations, such as water supply, dehydrated rations, emergency air bags (or, rather, carbon dioxide foam bags), and complete with high mobility joints (a problem with early spacesuits, which were as supple as boards) and some cunning features to cater for medical emergencies, such as tubular strips along arms and legs which - when activated - fills with a high-strength foam which quickly hardens to form splints for broken bones.

Why all the fuss? Well, the most important and costly resource of all on a remote colonising planet is people, and if you don't look after them, especially in conditions as severe as those on the surface of Mars, you'll soon be in trouble.

Aerial Residence

...such as flying houses, a seemingly daft idea which had taken root in my imagination as early as the first floating ones, and which Kevin and the rest of the FW development team positively salivated at the idea of; not that that guarantees anything... they and I soon discovered that it's even harder than it looks, although in principle it isn't a lot different from a very stable large-scale bloop. Obviously you have a lot more in the way of services, the comfort level needs to be pretty reliable, and the aerodynamics are a headache (akin to designing a flying brick, though people *can* get used to living in rounded rooms). I bounced the idea off my sponsors, who raised their collective eyebrows, but had been sufficiently enriched by my previous schemes to take a reasonably indulgent view. Flying houses only sound daft before you've considered some of the advantages, such as moving with the climate; being able to use water as a foundation and so avoiding hassles with land; getting out of the way of disasters, climatic and others (of which there are - not surprisingly - a large number these days); and not being inconvenienced by job changes (most people work on GN so I suppose this is a bit historical) or any of the other reasons for upping sticks. In fact it can get to sound positively attractive - at least it seemed so to me. None of this cut much ice with the sponsors but they coughed up enough to get me started anyway.

Having largely sorted the flight control and safety aspects got me off to a good start, but the engineering and control for the services was tricky, to say the least. The classic mobile home and it's more recent energy-saving, recycling, low-maintenance variants had solved many of the problems on a small scale, but when you need more heavy-duty systems to run continuously and reliably for years you tend to hit size problems - nobody wants a home as big (and smelly) as a combined water-purification plant, sewage works and power station etc. It would be like living on the edge of a small industrial estate. Miniaturisation isn't enough - by itself. Or redundancy. Or self-repair. But a judicious (and difficult to achieve) balance of all three, making best use of all the technologies that had been in continuous development since the twentieth century, combined with the ingenious electromechanical devices I'd put together for the bloops, sorted the problem - though initially at too high a cost, at least for the market I was supposed to be tackling.

That, by the way, was one of the conditions my sponsors slapped on me - no new development without a clear market in mind. Tedious, but necessary (at least to their peace of mind - I suppose I'd given them quite a few restless nights over the years), even though I suspected that this technology would create a new market all of its own. But they wouldn't have stood for that, so I invented a plausible-sounding niche and carried on (just for the record, it was for young, restless tekies, with minimal personal responsibilities, in high-level professional jobs, who, I theorised, would want the stimulation of physically moving around, bearing in mind that almost no-one actually had to go anywhere any more, given the wholly lifelike immediacy of high-bandwidth XR meetings).

I achieved some simple cost-cutting by shamelessly ripping off everything developed for bloops, especially the foams, where the material specs were not always perfect but generally good enough. Even so, I still found myself in the classic economic catch 22 of not being able to guarantee enough sales to bring unit prices down, which prices were too high to be sure of reasonable initial sales... Hmm... Well, as usual, it was FW to the rescue, Kevin and his teams' sim development efforts just needed a little tidying up and we let FW do the marketing for us, which it proceeded to do admirably. In no time we had flying virtual residences all over FW, which underwent a rapid social evolution, with numerous mobile enclaves, some of small-town size, including ocean-going and aerial versions, and with all sorts of attitudes and ideologies producing unique combinations of acceptance and expulsion rituals, written and unwritten rules and regulations, customs, stories, eccentricities, achievements; I was boggled by the speed at which the complexity developed, despite my familiarity with GN high-intensity life. What I also found intriguing was the comparison with the bloops, which had groups and clubs with their own ways of doing things, but on a much less grand scale. It seemed to me that if we put the resources into FW we could end up with full-blown flying or floating or peripatetic sim cities, with all the social and cultural paraphernalia that implied.

By this time (about a year and a half after selling the first FW flying house licenses) we had hordes of prospective customers almost beating the doors down to own the real thing - it was production time. The rest is history, as they say; with the high initial guaranteed sales (the aforementioned door-beaters-down) bringing down unit costs and hence prices, leading to higher sales, enabling prices to be further reduced, etc; i.e. the reverse of the original catch 22, though it wasn't a feedback loop that could continue for very long - just enough to significantly enhance my sponsors GN accounts yet again and make them receptive to some more of my blue-sky ideas, with the scepticism noticeably muted by now. Luckily - and I still don't know why - I developed some common-sense at this point, and realised there had to be limits on the profitability of further FW developments, so I restrained myself from immediately suggesting foamed space launchers or interstellar foam cruisers...

5 UP, UP AND AWAY!

***Mars tek** [5] - a better set of wheels...*

Getting about on Mars in the early days of colonisation poses some interesting problems. Mars' terrain isn't the easiest, with numerous extensive rock fields littered with rocks from two centimetres to twenty meters, plus fractured landscapes with a profusion of spectacular and terrifying chasms, cliffs and gorges, juxtaposed with huge, smooth plains with no identifying features, and, to add a little frisson should you feel things don't sound too bad so far, topped off with the peculiarly unstable surfaces of the poles, where out-gassing of water and carbon dioxide ices can turn innocent-looking surfaces into boiling maelstroms of dust, gases and fast-moving, sharp rocks. Not the sort of place you'd go for a pleasant, Sunday afternoon drive - unless your car was a little out of the ordinary...

Hard-won experience from early expeditions indicated the main requirements that a Mars all-terrain vehicle would have to satisfy (note we're only discussing one vehicle type here, the luxury of different types of vehicle suited to different terrains isn't an early priority). These requirements include being impervious to surface irregularities (large - very large - balloon tyres); unaffected by being turned over (central cabin mounted in a revolving frame attached to tyres so it flips over when the vehicle as a whole does, staying upright - though rather uncomfortable for any unstrapped cabin members...); all exterior surfaces highly abrasion-resistant - the perennial Mars requirement (foam tyres so big they take a long time to wear down, frame and cabin diamond-coated); independent, high-reliability power supply (hot rock generator with minimum fifty-year full-power output); ultra-high-reliability engines (most components made of diamond-coated high-strength foams), and multiple redundancy provided by having separate motors in all four wheels, any one of which can drive the rover alone at a pinch, if rather more slowly; all-weather protection and a high level of shock protection (floating suspension between cabin and frame), cabin tougher than most spacecraft and capable of being dropped from a greater height without significant damage than any hapless cabin inhabitants would be likely to survive - except that both vehicle and crew would be protected by the foam bags that would expand to absorb the impact before landing.

Plus a full set of living facilities in the cabin. In fact the (human driven) Mars rover is really a cross between a spacecraft and a tank that happens to spend its days perambulating across the surface of Mars.

The Challenge

Mind you, I hadn't developed *that* much common sense... Two things about space development gave me pause for thought, though: cost and danger. The cost of getting off the Earth and doing useful things in space had always proved exorbitant. One project alone, started at the end of the twentieth century, the International Space Station (ISS), swallowed a large proportion of the world's resources available for space development for quarter of a century. Various efforts to cheapen space projects had borne partial fruit - but had then run into the second big issue: danger. In particular, from the continual radiation that permeates space, which on Earth we're largely protected from by the atmosphere and magnetosphere. Living in space is an invitation to a short life terminated by radiation-induced cancers or other exotic diseases initiated by the tissue damage that radiation causes. Building shields capable of stopping most dangerous radiation had proved to be difficult, hideously expensive and frequently impracticable. But only allowing highly trained astronaut's short stays in space, to protect their health, is equally expensive and impracticable. Impasse. Satellites were OK, robots were OK, radiation-hardened Moon bases were OK. Radiation-hardened Mars bases were sort of OK, except that just getting to Mars was very, very expensive; which made Mars development, our best bet for a second bite of the cherry, planet-wise (the Moon hardly counted, it was OK for a short holiday but no fun to live on) very slow. And so Mars development had been plodding along now for over a century - not really getting anywhere and getting there slowly.

I'd been interested in this situation for years; various schemes for improving space travel or living had flitted through my over-active imagination, but the gap between these and implementation had always daunted my more practical engineering self. Now I saw my chance. I couldn't resist it, despite desperate screams from the aforementioned newly awakened common sense. I had very rich backers eating out of my hand, as well as substantial resources of my own (though, my practical self pointed out, these were pitiful compared with the sort of money governments routinely spent on the most minor of space ventures). What the hell. I took my XR-builder Kevin aside, who I knew was dying for a new challenge after the recent spate of mundane extensions to floating buildings, suggested a few ideas I'd been nurturing for some time now, and watched his eyes sparkle at the prospect. 'No probs boss' was his instant response as he headed back to his team to make a rather larger extension to FW than usual, and I headed back to my rig to develop the ideas to the degree of engineering detail necessary for a realistic sim. We were going to have fun.

At first glance foam, even the superfoams we'd been developing, seems strange stuff to build space modules with, but we'd done a whole lot of strange and unusual things with it, and we could now build foams to do heavy-duty work in some pretty hostile environments. Bulletproof foams as light as air were now commonplace. Ditto foams stronger than old-style reinforced concrete ('foamcrete', in fact) for building support skeletons for very large structures like floating towns, foamskins that reflected, deflected or absorbed a wide spectrum and power-range of radiation, transparent but UV-reflecting foams that could withstand pressurisation to usable levels in near-vacuum (developed for people who wanted to live above the weather). And so on - you get the idea. So I wasn't short of ready-made starting components to build interesting stuff like medium-altitude space stations with light enough gravity to minimise the cost of sending stuff into orbit or beyond. We'd also developed a lovely range of super-light-weight ion thrusters based on solar radiation (engines were another of my pet enthusiasms) - ideal to maintain structures in stable medium-altitude orbits where there was still enough air around to convert to high-speed ions. So that bit was easy.

The difficult bit was creating structures that could resist hard radiation beyond Earth's influence (not that I advertised such ambitions initially, of course - my sponsors weren't *that* stupid). There were two problems to be solved here: the availability of materials (carting large quantities of stuff into orbit had always been a killer for large-scale space projects); and the difficulty of constructing things in space (this had proved one of the bugbears of the ISS). I set about solving both with the teks developed in FW. Firstly, near-space orbits, i.e. orbits that graze the atmosphere, are not devoid of materials. Far from it. In particular there's CHON, which you can - with a little ingenuity - build lots of interesting stuff from (and do everyone a favour into the bargain by removing some excess carbon dioxide). Then there's space debris, removal of which would not only provide you with lots of interesting materials but do everyone an even bigger favour by making space a safer place (and Earth too, in a rather smaller way). Catching space debris is a hard thing to do usually, but we weren't constrained by the usual limitations - putting a stop to the carefree high-speed lifestyle of such debris by putting very large chunks of foam in their path was child's-play to us. So at least we had some fairly substantial on-site building materials.

Next stop: construction. Building large, intricate structures out of foam was something we'd been doing for quite some time now. OK, not in microgravity or near-vacuum, and with somewhat easier access to tools and production facilities, but building large, floating structures was something we could do. So we did. First in FW, developing versions of XR space tourism and edutainment with our inimitable foam twist, and then - after our backers had gulped a few times at the costs and twisted a few arms to get a little government money involved too (well, OK, quite a lot, actually...) - for real.

Mars tek [6] - the answer lies in the soil...

If human beings want to stay somewhere a long time then they need to have food - but not just any food: Earth food. That is, food more or less exactly equivalent to food grown/raised on Earth.

Chemically produced food or food derived from simple organisms like algae are fine for short periods or even, with supplements, moderately long periods - but you can't raise new generations on them without significant health problems. The reason for this is reasonably well known, or at least intelligently guessed at, as a lack of a range and balance of micro-nutrients, many of them known but not all, and most of them associated with or affected by the soil in which the food or feed plants are grown. The upshot is you have to grow at least some food as near to Earth conditions as you can get, at least as far as the quality of the soil is concerned.

In other words, you need the muck and bugs and worms that so gloriously combine to make good rich Earth soils. What this means in practice is that you have to take a little piece of Earth with you wherever you go, literally and not just figuratively. This in turn means that for long journeys - and the only short space journey we can make, apart from going into orbit around the Earth itself, is to the Moon - we have to either build and maintain space greenhouses or use a very sophisticated suitcase that soil can be happily transported in. It's prudent to do both, in fact, as you can't afford to lose your soil base in a greenhouse accident. So, of all people, soil scientists are amongst the most important when establishing remote colonies, and on top of the multifarious luggage and equipment which you can stow away and forget about you have this collection of precious and fragile dirt that needs to be kept happy for a long time in pretty extreme conditions.

Once you get where you're going you have to multiply your relatively small soil base, even if you're only going to use soil-grown food as a supplement. On Mars a mix of dust, ground-up rock and fast-growing organics from hydroponics tanks can be used as a matrix to expand the population of worms and bugs and other soil organisms - plant and animal - which characterise good old-fashioned Earth loam. Of course, you also take along a host of potential diseases and parasites, but nothing's perfect.

Spaced

We started small (that is, if you call a geostationary space station
the size of a small town, small), mainly to test the tek for materials
production and get our construction people used to working in
even nearer space conditions than they were already. Once we'd
got the bugs out of the new foam manufacturing processes and had
a sensible place to live (with effective radiation shields of ten-
meter-thick reflective/deflective foam) we were in business. The
space construction business. We gradually bootstrapped ourselves
up to serious production capacities, and as we did so the pressure
of would-be tourists, colonists, explorers, media hacks, and so on
and so forth, grew inexorably. As the old saying goes, nothing
succeeds like excess, and we were now producing serious
quantities of radiation-resistant foam, high-pressure dome foam,
high-strength structural foam, foam solar panels and recycling
plants and greenhouses and...

People (and corporations, large and small, and governments)
bought our stock and they bought our products. We sold our
activities as space opera and, as it was for real, we no longer
needed to sim the action. We sold ringside seats to wealthy tourists
and put satellites into orbit for peanuts, short-circuiting most of the
environmental problems into the bargain. I knew the honeymoon
would be over soon enough and we needed to make real money
and cut long-term risks. In particular we needed to decentralise and
diversify so that when the inevitable accidents and major problems
arose, as they generally did on such humongous large and complex
projects eventually, we wouldn't have all our eggs broken at once.
This costs more, of course (it's nearly always cheaper to expand
production at an existing facility than to build a new one). That's

what I used the honeymoon for, to get unpopular (usually because of cost) decisions passed. After four and a half hard years I had three high-atmosphere geostationary plants going strong, albeit the most recent still in the thick of construction; we could efficiently inject satellites into a wide range of orbits (if a little more slowly than conventional rockets and space-planes); attached to each plant we had a space hotel/entertainment complex, one fully operational, one almost complete and already in use, and the third designed and started building; we had two Earth-Moon cruisers running a regular schedule (and providing us with a new source of materials) and stimulating Moonbase development as never before; and we had more lucrative edutainment contracts than we knew what to do with (figuratively speaking, though there was never any shortage of uses for the money).

Most important of all, both to me and to the growing band of experienced space engineers, was the undisputed fact that we now had tested tek to make it all work reliably. We were making - and spending - fortunes, but getting results without cutting ridiculously dangerous corners. We felt that, at long last, space tek was coming of age. At this point a sensible person would have drawn breath and consolidated, letting things settle down a little. Reviewed activities and progress to date to understand the situation better before embarking on more perilous ventures.

Fat chance.

Mars tek [7] - the energy game(1)...

Energy. Plenty of it on Earth of course, especially when you have modern low-energy tek and distributed energy generation. But Mars (surprise surprise) is different: no fossil fuels (not that we get to use them these days, but they gave us a start); less sun -

Mars is further from the sun and continent-wide (sometimes planet-wide) dust storms can obscure it for long, unpredictable periods - and so less energy is available for all potential renewable energy sources; and no geothermal, at least none near enough to the surface to be practicably accessible. Of course you could beam energy down from orbiting solar power stations (though those dust storms would still get in the way unless you used some clever transmission teks), but then you'd be starting off with a very complicated and centralised energy system, which would be colossally expensive to build, run and maintain.

Discounting the last option and totting up the renewables quickly leads you to an unpalatable conclusion: you can't generate enough energy from natural resources on Mars to build and run an expanding colony, at least in the early stages. The sums simply don't add up, at least not if you assume the colony is to become self-supporting in a reasonable time span - which you have to, pretty much, because the cost of just getting there and down to the surface in one piece is gob-smackingly high enough. Which only leaves one option (apart from staying at home, that is): nuclear.This is a very difficult option, unfortunately, though not so much for the tek as the politics. Nuclear energy has had a bad press on Earth for a long time, mostly deserved it has to be said, what with large areas of land and sea-bed left too radioactive for use for centuries, and the massive semi-stable dumps of highly radioactive waste dotting the Earth's surface...

Mars?

I felt I had to go for the big one while I was still riding the wave. I'd already put together with Kevin, my XR genius, a secret version of FW which included the heavy-duty deep-space cruisers necessary for the long voyage to Mars. My God, were they expensive... despite desperately sticking as close as possible to proven - or at least used once - tek, *and* assuming the Mars' recruits would be dedicated enough to not mind the absence of frills... that is, *very* dedicated indeed... In theory, of course, there was already a Mars base, run by robots (though set up by a couple of even more than usually intrepid groups of people who'd endured several very unpleasant years to do so). But I wasn't betting there'd be a lot working by the time we got there (I sort of daydreamed of going in person and included myself in the 'we' - but I knew the bastards wouldn't let me go).

Mars wasn't so much a testing ground as a breaking ground, you got anywhere near the place and half your stuff immediately stopped working. I know that sounds superstitious but it seemed to be borne out by experience. Perhaps everyone had just been unlucky so far... then again, perhaps they were underestimating the magnitude of the task and just trusting in luck; it wouldn't have been the first time major space missions had been sent out on a wing and a prayer - only Mars is too tough to get away with that sort of wishful thinking. Whatever, I wasn't taking any more chances than I had to: there may have been no frills but there *were* a lot of tools; everything was engineered tough, with plenty of spares; all the electronics was self-repairing; prime functions like water and air extraction / treatment / recycling were duplicated several different ways. You get the picture. We knew enough about Martian geochemistry to turn the rock into foamcrete, and we knew how to coat the exposed portions so they wouldn't get whittled down by the Martian sandblasting winds. Plus we had foam fabrication tek down to a fine art and could build just about anything out of the stuff. We were as ready as we would ever be: I tentatively proposed the project to my sponsors...

...that took the smile off their faces. They asked me for the figures; I lied and said we only had the tek assessments at this stage - I just wanted their reaction (this last bit was true). They did their homework on the state (and, more to the point, the cost) of Mars exploration so far, and came back and said that was a good joke. Not a great joke, but a good one. At this point my earlier misgivings returned to haunt me - getting funding wasn't going to be any easier than it had ever been... I replied that it was no joke, though I didn't expect them to pick up the full tab. So who was... perhaps I would like to explain my funding strategy in a little more detail?..

My strategy had three main parts: firstly we put a strong tek case (already complete) to the controllers of the existing Mars programme (who I knew were already scratching around for a new approach with *some* chance of success) to get a chunk of the huge resources they had access to; secondly we market the same case (minus some tek detail and plus some neat frills) to the great stock-owning public, to spread a little risk elsewhere; thirdly, and finally, we put in a reasonable portion of the wealth we'd (i.e. me and my sponsors) already accrued from the previous highly successful (I rubbed this bit in) FW ventures. Of course I knew they would interpret my idea of 'reasonable' as 'extortionate', but we were into some heavy bargaining here and I had to set a sensible start position. This was going to take some time. I wasn't too concerned, because setting up and sim testing the new equipment in the no-longer-secret Mars FW was pretty exhausting and time-consuming anyway. Unfortunately my backers were taking a similar attitude towards the financing of the venture. Unless I came up with some good wheezes (sorry, 'reasons') to persuade both them and the other parties that there was money to be made, I'd be ricocheting backwards and forwards between them for some considerable time to come. Indefinitely, in fact. Hmm...

I soon realised that a rational approach would get me nowhere fast - I needed some good PR, not to say outright propaganda, to persuade enough people to act against their own best interests to get the project off the ground. As it were. I mentally ticked off the numerous PR people I'd encountered during the rise of my FW empire. Some were good, one or two were very good, but I couldn't quite seem to fix on one who was so good they could pull off the miracle of imaginative advertising I suspected I needed. There was also a further difficulty to identifying the best snake-oil merchant in town, which was that the Mars project was a necessarily long-term one, so it was no good the image collapsing half-way there, I needed the story to retain its credibility at least until the first ship arrived and got its act together, at which point even a modicum of success would buoy the whole enterprise up. Despite my earlier attitude I realised that I didn't have a lot of time to resolve the issue, any obvious delay on my part and the interested parties would start drifting away (or, rather, running away as fast as their short, fat, hairy little legs could carry them). I began to wonder if what I needed wasn't a real miracle, a prospect that even my elevated self-confidence faltered at...

Mars tek [8] - the energy game(2)...

Thanks to the bad nuclear press the lobby for a pristine Mars, unsullied by nuclear activities, was a pretty solid one. However, when it became clear that without nuclear power it would be 'look but don't touch' more or less indefinitely, ways and means of producing nuclear power without the dis-benefits of previous approaches were investigated. It was clear from the start that building large-scale nuclear power plants on Mars wasn't feasible; nor, for that matter, was the construction of continental distribution grids. It had to be distributed nuclear power, an alien concept to nuclear designers, for whom the dangers of nuclear materials always dictated some form of closely-controlled and centralised facilities.

The impasse was overcome by the development of 'hot rocks'; small cores of highly radioactive material embedded in super-strong radiation-resistant ceramic 'pebbles' that constantly absorbed the radiation and gave off copious amounts of heat which - depending on the pebble size relative to the radioactive core - varied in surface temperature from the red heat needed to drive a small generator to the mild warmth that would maintain the temperature of a hot water tank. The mix of radionuclides was calculated to produce a constant output for as long a time as the rock's ceramics were expected to reliably withstand the internal and external stresses they'd be continually subjected to - centuries for cooler rocks and high decades for the hottest (though the design allowed for hotter rocks to continue to function as cooler ones for a while thereafter).

A spin-off was the potential to convert Earth's high-level radioactive waste to useful energy - the ultimate in recycling. The purists charged politicians with dumping waste on Mars (despite the fact that most hot rocks would be used on Earth) but the - by now common - knowledge that there were no other practical options to kick-start Mars colonisation caused their cries to fall on deaf ears. Every Mars base would need its share of hot rocks if it was to have a viable starting level of energy production.

Emergency

It's funny how things turn up in the most unlikely ways at times (or so it seems afterwards, I suppose). I was staring morosely at the space news feed one evening, mostly composed of items generated by my own activities, something which usually gave me a warm, self-congratulatory feeling but, at that moment, merely rubbed in my inability to get any further. Then an item came up which startled me out of my dejected self-pity: a Chinese spaceship on route to Mars, whose existence wasn't even generally known (it wasn't to me and I thought I knew *everything* about current Mars projects) was in difficulties, a meteorite hit or major engine failure of some sort (at this stage they were still cagey about admitting anything). It would still make it to Mars and - with difficulty - get into a rather wide (but rapidly decaying...) orbit around it. But there it would stay (well, for a while...). It couldn't land and it couldn't leave. I sincerely thanked the Chinese government for their (insufficient) efforts, and set about contacting the best of the PR people I'd identified, to put together a heart-warming story of the great efforts and sacrifices of the hapless men and women on the Chinese ship and how we could collectively rescue them - something which would have been impossible without the serendipitous development of a Mars plan by FW enterprises... I'm sorry if that sounds cynical, believe it or not I felt genuine concern for the Chinese astronauts, but you can't blame me (well, you can if you like, I suppose) for seeing this event as manna from heaven.

It would be a very close thing, though, even if it was possible. In theory the Chinese vessel had closed-cycle recycling of air, water and nutrients, which would enable them to survive indefinitely. In current practice things ran out in fairly short order on anything smaller than a small planet. Their chances of not running out of something essential before the minimum two and a half years it would take us to get to them were slim. Fortunately I had seen that straight away and had gone into a frenzy of activity to get things moving at maximum throttle. Even more fortunately my outsize ego had prompted me to get construction started on the main vessel even before I had agreement from the parties I'd ultimately need to squeeze the money out of. That's one good reason why I was sweating at the lack of enthusiasm for the project, of course... But now having everything thundering forward was the only chance the Chinese astronauts would see us in close enough proximity to rescue them rather than waving us sadly goodbye on the comslink as they expired while we were still only half way.

The whole world bought my stock, governments voted large chunks of their space budgets ditto, and - after carefully assessing the magnitude of the response and hence reduction in personal risk (the bastards) - my main sponsors put their hands in their pockets and completed the circle. I smiled cheerily as I stood with them in the group video footage being transmitted to the main news-feeds, while gritting my teeth and wishing I had my hands around their necks, but that's showbiz for you.

The trick now was good financial control; we had pots of money, perhaps enough even for a Mars trip... but we couldn't spend it all at once and I had to keep an eagle eye on where it was going during the long and complex preparations for the voyage. I didn't want to delay by a moment going to rescue the Chinese ship, I genuinely felt for them, but neither did I want to run a simple rescue and return (or, worse still, send out an inadequate expedition that would end up simply joining them in their plight). So I had to get all the multifarious sub-projects of Martian colonisation tek running simultaneously and ensure they finished in time to be loaded on the rescue vessel. Put simply, it was an intensely exciting nightmare. This conflict - between getting under way ASAP and preparing for a major colonisation expedition - would have sunk the whole enterprise if I hadn't already had FW enterprises working flat out on the latter. Even so I had a problem: it was obvious to me that world opinion, on which I was dependent in more ways than one, would turn against me if I stalled for time in order to get the engineering fully together. So I found a way to have my cake and eat it...

...in essence, I packed the tools to make the machines rather than the machines themselves. This was where the big advantage of foam tek really counted - that it gives you the best possible ratio of material resources to resultant artefacts. In other words, you can make a lot of stuff out of not very much - and we now knew how to build almost anything out of varieties of foam. The downside was we'd have to send some of our best foam engineers on the journey, so losing their skills to the burgeoning near-Earth space industry (because of the coms delays between Earth and Mars it was impractical to run things remotely). So be it, if we were successful then Mars development would be on its way at last, and the loss to the industry closer to home could soon be made up. Of course, if we weren't...

Before we could get the re-vamped enterprise under way, however, we had a serious problem to solve, which was that the tools for making and manipulating foams were too large. On Earth, or even floating in near-space, size wasn't a critical issue, though for the latter we'd already had to shrink and lighten some of the machinery. Luckily (again... though *I* put it down to foresight) I'd already initiated a project to miniaturise foam-handling equipment (I actually had in mind the possibility of distributed facilities, so that remote communities could make and maintain foam artefacts). The project wasn't as far along as I would have liked but it got some hefty acceleration as soon as I realised what was needed. So, in short order, there were projects to shrink foam machinery, build the huge foam anti-radiation envelope needed to protect expedition members, manufacture the many massive foam girders and panels for the vehicle superstructure, accumulate the materials for building foam equipment in transit, and so on and so forth, ad nauseam.

6 THE RESCUE

Mars tek [9] - *hello, hello, is anybody there?..*

Contrary to a lot of popular sci-fi one of the first things a new colony needs to do on reaching the planet of their choice is reinforce their space capability. You don't land on the planet and cannibalise your spacecraft for farm equipment or whatever. Far from it - you need access to space, in particular for coms, more than ever (unless the planet is such an Eden that you can more or less abandon hi-tek and live idyllically off the land - fat chance). An early priority of Mars expeditions with serious colonising intent is to establish planet-wide coms, including a minimal (but still extremely capable) version of Earth's GN network - Mars GN, or M-GN. Half of the would-be colonists need to stay in the sky (that is, low Mars orbit) and get stuck into satellite-building, including remote sensing satellites to produce detailed maps of the Mars surface and sub-surface, and into building reliable long-distance space-based transport and emergency energy resources based on very-large-scale solar arrays. Once you're in space, leaving it altogether is a very stupid thing to do.

M-GN provides would-be Martians with an information system to make the most of Mars' limited resources. Once the net's in place you can never be lost; interactive or emergency auto remotes ensure your position can be known to the system at any time, or at least (if you fall down a very deep crack) your approximate position from your last recorded signal. But M-GN is a lot more than a handy person locater, it's the embodiment of many decades of GN developments in information processing, with sims, schedulers and infrastructure control in general - not that Mars would have much infrastructure to start with, but what it did have it would need to use very efficiently indeed. Plus - a big plus to modern humans - M-GN with all its coms and sims and apps and info and facilities makes a place seem more like home.

Frenetic

To their credit, once the secret was out (and the various world governments had satisfied their need for ritual posturing), the Chinese government made all the specifications of their expedition available to us to analyse for potential problems and, hopefully, solutions. Unfortunately it quickly became apparent that the crew weren't going to survive the two and a half years it would take us to get to them. At best, assuming we and they proved resourceful enough to tackle the worst of the immediate problems, they might last two years. I convened a high-level meeting of the world's best space engineers to bat a few ideas around. It seemed there was really only one option: we had to build *two* long-range vehicles, one manned (i.e. the main one, which we were already building) and one not, the latter containing enough of the missing ingredients to tide the Chinese over the extra six months it would take the main vessel to get to them. It was a knotty problem; without people we could accelerate the second vessel pretty much as hard as we liked (assuming it wasn't going to hold too much delicate equipment) - except that it needed stopping at the other end, too... it would be frustrating, to say the least, to watch your life-saving supply ship zoom past at a quarter light-speed or whatever...

In the end we got a rough and ready first solution that would save us six months, with pretty wasteful use of fuel despite making the most of the various planetary bodies involved for extra free acceleration and braking. We gave it to the detailed sim people to hone as best they could. This part of the exercise was where we found the sudden investment bounty very handy. Basically we just went out and bought booster rockets like they were going out of fashion (they were) and other bits of proven space tek (remember, we weren't going to have a lot of time to work on this in situ as it was going to be speeding ahead of us most of the time) and lashed them together, using unbelievable quantities of sim time in the worlds best space sims to get the best build in the least time with a reasonably low risk (there are no zero-risk options in space). It was exciting stuff - though the Chinese crew limping in a decaying orbit around Mars might have seen it differently.

As the launch date approached things became rapidly more frenetic. We got into the usual 'tools to make the tools to make the tools' loop, running sims all over the place to ensure we could - practically as well as theoretically - make all the artefacts we'd need on arrival. There would be no question of anyone sitting around bored in the two years to Mars (the two and a half years included the six months to get everything together - itself an almost impossible deadline), the poor bastards would be working flat out all the way... not much of a problem with in-flight entertainment then... At the start I had resolved to think big and ensure the resources were available to make it all work properly (notice I didn't say 'smoothly') on arrival. My engineers - even though they were used to my eccentric visions by now - had thought I'd finally lost it when I presented my initial ideas, including a vehicle ten kliks across. Now we found it was only just big enough... unfortunately I was too frantically busy to walk about with a smug 'I told you so' smile on my face, but you can't have everything.

When I thought about it afterwards I realised that an amazing thing had happened: the whole world had pulled together and given its best shot at saving those Chinese astronauts. Despite the antipathy that existed between various national governments and the niggling annoyance with the Chinese government for trying to pull a fast one and gain a secret toehold on Mars (the Chinese realised in due course that even 'toehold' was too grand a term for what they would have achieved, even without the accident); despite the truly mind-boggling cost and the improbability of getting any return on the investment; despite the fact that tens of thousands of people were dying of starvation, preventable disease and war every single month; despite all these and other factors everybody - or at least a very large proportion of everybody - still wanted the hapless Chinese astronauts to be saved. I wondered afterwards if the frustration at the failure of our attempts so far at Mars development wasn't a major factor in the response. After the relatively easy successes of the early Moon shots, and later Moon bases, the sheer hardness of getting anywhere with Mars was a rude awakening to the awesome difficulty of real space colonisation. It seemed to me that here was a genuine case of the collective unconscious at work, that humankind en masse was frustrated with the signal lack of success on Mars, which had rubbed our collective noses in the inadequacy and fragility of our space tek. Basically, we all wanted to see a success for once, to feel good about the capability of our species, and feel some optimism about the future.

Well, something like that.

Mars tek *[10] - waste not want not...*

On Mars recycling is not a luxury: there are no rubbish dumps, no waste pits, no litter. Everything except rocks is too precious to leave lying around. Future archaeologists had better hope they can glean enough from the electronic record because there won't be much else apart from the paraphernalia of the current (or last...) society, and some holes in the ground. Every scrap of foam, metal, solid plastic, clothes, uneaten food and just about everything else, has a recycling plan. Anything that doesn't easily recycle has its design, build or materials modified until it does. All CHON and life-based materials - sewage, food waste, plant waste etcetera - are recycled through bacterial digesters or simple composting.

Earth used to go through regular phases of planned or unplanned obsolescence - Mars designs for permanence, with recycling at the end. This approach has certain advantages, such as ending materials shortages fairly quickly, even rare metals don't remain in short supply for long, as their production, even at low levels, is cumulative because so little is lost from the system. Another is effective use of labour; utilities, manufacturing and services are all geared to long-term efficiency, so time otherwise wasted on unnecessary processing of rapidly obsolescent goods and ephemeral fashion-driven skills are largely avoided, unless there is a general consensus otherwise. This naturally leads to a two-tier system in which two economies operate: the first maintains the basic infrastructure, goods and services necessary for day-to-day life, while the second caters for more esoteric tastes - though still within the recycling ethos.

A part, or extension, of this second tier is really a separate, third, tier, that embodies the sort of long-term aims and spiritual values that in previous ages built pyramids and cathedrals. On Mars this finds expression in the continuation of the outward expansion, increasing the sphere of human influence, rather than converting mountains into monuments, and requires the best possible use to be made of whatever resources are available. On a planet where nothing comes for free you have to make such spare capacity from every scrap and ounce of material and effort left over from day to day living.

Launches

It was the big day, the best launch window we could cobble together at such short notice. Nothing, but nothing, was actually finished (well, I suppose the ion drives had to be...). But our sims said we could get everything together with what we had, and that's what counted. I marvel at times at the power of XR. The main vehicle - the Hope (well, what else?) - was actually bigger than the largest of the space stations, which gives an indication of the scale of the enterprise (numerous wags had suggested just fitting a few motors to a station, but of course it would just have broken up under the strain, as per the following). Moving such large objects poses considerable problems, as the propulsive forces have to be very carefully balanced to avoid having half of it going in one direction and the other half in another, with lots of crinkly broken bits in-between... As with all complex space vehicles this one was inhabited by a powerful SAI with a shed-full of sensors and actuators at its beck and call. In fact the SAI was powerful enough to have interesting conversations with - when it wasn't busy with the ship, that is.

The Mars rescue (/colonisation...) mission was the greatest media feeding frenzy of all time. Real-time interactive XR was a non-starter, the Hope was out of range for immediate responses in short order, but even with this limitation the opportunities for exploiting the constant stream of data being beamed back seemed limitless. In effect the whole of Earth's entertainment industry (now the biggest industry by almost any measurement) took on a different spin for the duration of the trip, and I don't think things have been the same since. Sci-fi (or, rather, Sci-fact...) became main stream, big time. I believe that the sheer scale, excitement and chutzpah of the voyage and its subsequent developments did something to the whole planet. But then, I would say that, wouldn't I, being the prime mover...

Certainly nobody could sensibly deny the enormous impact on the world of that voyage, an optimism and energy enveloped it and everything associated with it. I seriously began to wonder when I was going to reach my collapse point from sheer overwork, I hardly seemed to sleep for the whole two and a half years, with the momentum increased even more nine months after launch with the launch (from the Hope) of the high-speed second vehicle ('Rescuer' - not a lot of imagination invested there, either). The sims had shown that this approach gave the best trajectory, launching Rescuer from the Hope when the latter was close to its maximum speed. The only way to compress time to arrival by the necessary six months was to up the speed of Rescuer to the point where stopping at the other end would be a chancy business indeed, using both gravity and atmospheric braking via Mars to bring the ship into an extreme elliptical orbit. As there were no astronauts on board - something that had been agreed in the teeth of vehement opposition from the world's media, who would have given their collective right arms for photo opportunities of rescuing astronauts personally greeting their Chinese counterparts - it was feasible to allow higher g forces, atmospheric braking turbulence and temperatures etc. and hence, hopefully, arrive in time.

Mars tek *[11] - remodelings and makeovers...*

Before we established a permanent presence on Mars there was no shortage of grand plans to terraform it into a miniature Earth, complete with an atmosphere and an ocean (well, a sea or two anyway). Once there, the sheer difficulty of large-scale engineering of all kinds on Mars, especially of the type typical of Earth involving thousands or tens of thousands of skilled people, made such blue-sky plans seem laughable, certainly for the foreseeable future. No-one denies, though, that we're already transforming, if not terraforming, Mars; it's now a considerably more human-friendly place - even the atmosphere is showing signs of thickening, despite the best efforts at recycling air and water, so it's no longer inconceivable that human activities may eventually thicken the atmosphere enough to breathe - by our standards, that is, equivalent to the top of Everest.

There is no flowing water or plant growth outside of caves and greenhouses yet, nor will there be for some time to come, but we've already developed experimental bacteria and lichens that can almost live unprotected on the Martian surface, and, given the aforementioned atmospheric thickening, they'll be ready to try out soon. In a few decades or so. This is the difference between Earthbound theory and Martian fact: we Martians are happy with the way things are developing, we've adapted to conditions that would have been unbearable to our forbears on Earth, and that's what characterises human beings after all - adaptability. We'd like better conditions but we're prepared to wait as long as it takes and, in the meantime, use a very advanced and pragmatic tek to supply our needs and make life more than just bearable. We may seem a tough, dour bunch to you more fragile Earthlings, but appearances, as they say, are deceptive; we're doing things we find meaningful and fulfilling and interesting (and fun), and what better definition of happiness is there than that?

Slowdown

It was, as they say, a close-run thing. The voyage of the Hope itself wasn't without incident, in fact a considerable number of incidents, indeed a full-blown soap opera that I'd swear had been arranged by the media themselves if I hadn't known better. It was inevitable that many things would happen, given the extreme intensity of activity of a lot of very talented (and, I'd say, over-sexed - but I suppose that's sour grapes) people in a very complex environment. Really, the Hope was more like a sizeable manufacturing town, a frontier town at that, than a space-going vessel; any ideas anyone might have had about quiet professionalism and clinically clean and tidy work areas were dispelled in the first thirty seconds of broadcasting of scenes from the interior. It was huge, messy and incredibly busy; contained more tek than many small nations; and had a development schedule that would have made Henry Ford's hair curl. This last was because - as already mentioned - there simply hadn't been time to put everything together in Earth orbit, and there'd be no spare time when they got to Mars. If they didn't climb the learning curve and get basic needs - air, water, food, shelter - sorted in a very short time after arrival, they'd be lucky to even get back.

So how did we manage to provide all the media fodder then? Good question (if rhetorical). It came down to a choice between having a Big Brother battery of cams and recorders - remotes - everywhere, or allowing media teams on the trip. The latter was a non-starter, the extra load alone - given that we already had more engineers on board than originally intended - vetoed it. So they had to put up with Big Brother. I'd had visions of typically sneaky tekies 'accidentally' sabotaging the recording equipment and not finding the time to repair it in their hyper-busy schedule; so I personally warned all senior people before the launch that the remotes had to be kept going at all cost, we might as well stay at home as far as the colonisation restart was concerned if we didn't get the spondulics from media coverage. They grumbled but they got the message. We made sure no-one else could intercept the data by flying a large relay station to capture and kill the tight-beam signal before it got anywhere near Earth, and we charged for access to all the many data-feeds by the second. The total annual value of all the feeds was a number so large I had difficulty comprehending - never mind believing - it. This media value alone almost financed the whole project (I only said 'almost'...).

Anyway, back to the rescue. The only way the Chinese could survive even the two years to the high-speed fly-by would be by putting almost all of them into hibernation or some other low-energy state. The means of doing this for real hadn't been perfected yet, though some good approximations existed. The major problem is that the human body is a high energy device, it doesn't readily tolerate being shut down - or even appreciably slowed - for extended periods. But it *can* be done, witness the Indian Yogi's who can be buried for months at a time and survive by slowing their metabolism - especially their heart rate and brain energy use - close to a standstill. Unfortunately we didn't have ten years or so to train the Chinese crew in these techniques... Except that we (or, rather, they) got lucky, in that one of their number *did* have the relevant Yoga training - it's not uncommon in China - so we had something to build on. Their crew also included a top-flight biochemist and a couple of good medicos; so we and they put together a strategy that utilised all of these skills plus what tek they had to address the problem of having too many people for the available food, water and oxygen for the two years.

Basically, we slowed as many people down as possible for as much time as we could safely achieve, using a combination of meditation and drug-induced sleep and near-sleep states. The best we found we could safely achieve for that length of time was an average metabolic consumption of about four hundred calories a day, which, with some Heath-Robinson repairs to their greenhouses and algae vats and an acceptable average weight loss, barely scraped into the two year time frame. We all knew, including the Chinese, that these calculations incorporated an unreasonably optimistic view of events between then and now, but there was nothing else we could do, or so we thought then. Except pray.

Mars tek *[12] - red green fingers...*

Plants can do odd things on Mars, it's easy to forget on Earth how sensitive and reactive to their environment plants are, and growing in the very different conditions of even the pressurised cave greenhouses on Mars throws up surprises. A major difference between Earth and Mars, one that we can do nothing about, is the gravity. Different plants react differently to this; some grow bigger, some grow in different ways to their counterparts on Earth, such as developing huge proliferations of leaves but no flowers, or sending out roots from odd places as if a third Earth gravity isn't enough for some plants to know which way is up. Add the other differences such as those in the light spectrum and intensity (using Earth-normal sunlamps isn't really an option for mass agriculture) and the reconstituted atmosphere (at lower pressure as well) and you have a recipe for botanical homesickness which can have numerous and unexpected effects - including the production of new or elevated levels of existing toxins or, conversely, failure to produce nutrients that their Earthbound cousins have no problems supplying in abundance.

Fortunately we were aware there might be such problems from the start and tested the food rigorously before we ate it - which turned out to be a wise move indeed. Some foods could be adjusted, others had to be temporarily abandoned (once we had the gene tek up and running more extensive adjustments were possible), or used for other purposes than those originally intended. It was an interesting lesson on the effects of new environments and made some of us wonder if we too would be subject to side-effects in the long run... But, just as the majority of plants turned out to be more or less ok, with a few minor eccentricities of growth and form, the majority of people have too, so we cross our collective fingers and hope that this initial adjustment of both plants and people is enough to start us on the path of a more long-term adaptation which will see both us and our artefacts, both living and tek, more-or-less safely into the wide open spaces beyond the Earth.

Rescuer

As I've already said, it was a close-run thing. Six months to the intercept with Rescuer we agreed with the Chinese crew to put them all onto a more extreme drug regime that would take them as close to real hibernation as we dared go, which had never been done before, leaving the one guy with Yoga training on meditation only and enough food so he'd actually be able to move when Rescuer arrived. Ideally the intercept should have been handled by robots, but the Chinese hadn't equipped their ship with anything powerful enough, probably for the same reason we hadn't put one on Rescuer, namely to save the extra weight and complexity of a robot and its maintenance gear. So this poor guy, half starved and knowing beforehand that the chances of failure were probably better than evens, constituted the single-handed reception committee for Rescuer.

Not that he could afford to hang around, like reception committees generally do, as there was an awful lot of things to keep tabs on, though he had a very able helper in the shape of Rescuer's SAI, which was almost as good as the one on Hope (plus some pretty good ones of their own - you're never alone any more, whoever and wherever you are). Rescuer only had minimal sensors and remotes, though the SAI made good use of what it had during the journey; once the intercept was imminent, however, the SAI had to pay attention to that, leaving more ordinary processors (still pretty powerful, even so) to deal as best they could with media coverage. That we could even spare a thought for such a thing in such a dire emergency indicates the momentousness of the occasion; everybody, the Chinese astronauts included, recognised the importance of having the Earth's population aware of and supporting everything that happened on this twin (triple, with Rescuer) voyage to Mars. Without this there was the chance that Martian development would be left to wither and eventually be abandoned indefinitely, perhaps blighting the chances for humankind of any future in space. This probably sounds rather over-dramatised, but, knowing what I know now, I don't think so: I believe we came within a squeak of giving up on space, and if I do nothing else with my life I shall feel it was worthwhile just for having helped overcome that defeatism.

Rescuer went past the Chinese ship like a streak of lightning on the first pass, as expected. The braking manoeuvre required to halt its progress was extreme and hair-raising - the ship went so close to the Martian surface its skin got dust abrasion. It missed a couple of high points by literally a few meters, and the impact of the tortured Martian atmosphere on them, despite its thinness, must have been truly spectacular - unfortunately, we didn't get any visuals other than a grainy long-distance one from what was left of the Chinese sensors (though, personally, I still think it's pretty impressive, though I suppose I'm easily pleased) - our own were inoperative, of course, as Rescuer was encased in a white-hot plasma of ablating atmospheric shield. Ah well, you can't have everything.

Even after this fly-by, which was about as close to a fly-into as you can get without actually doing it, it was touch and go whether the braking had been enough to get Rescuer into a usable orbit - we all cheered like lunatics when the info came back that it had. But only just. And even that at the cost of some heat damage to the cargo; the ablative foam shield had been totally burnt away in the Martian atmosphere. The SAI had even had to use some of the fuel mass as coolant, which left precious little margin for subsequent corrective manoeuvres. It had to leave the Chinese to their own devices for an extra five days, despite knowing that every hour was crucial, due to the resultant lack of fuel. When we discovered how close we were to failure we stopped cheering and started nail-biting...

The lone (awake, that is) Chinese astronaut was close to his limits by the time Rescuer returned, and it didn't help that he had to do some additional manoeuvring of the Chinese vessel, which was both difficult and a risk to the viability of the ship during the six months it still had to hang together until the cavalry, i.e. us, arrived. To say that he surpassed himself is an understatement of some magnitude; he managed, with the SAIs, to get the two ships together and revive nearly all the crew. Two of them, both men, were seriously ill, they'd reacted badly to the powerful home-made hibernation drugs. So as soon as we found we'd succeeded in getting aid to them, we also discovered we had a medical emergency on our hands. I don't like to sound cynical, but I'm sure the media were delighted with the drama.

The SAI we'd sent, once fully integrated with the Chinese ship, used its medical software, in conjunction with the detailed physio records usually kept on astronauts, and with the help of one of the Chinese medicos (the other was one of the ill men, unfortunately), to produce a medical programme for them that was probably as good as anything on Earth, but we couldn't save both. One recovered reasonably well, if slowly, but the other deteriorated and eventually sank into a deep coma. We hung in there with him for a while, until it became clear he wasn't going to recover any time soon, and he was using a lot of scarce resources. We left the final decision to his Captain and crew-mates (and, presumably, the Chinese government), but we all knew that the delay increased the distinct possibility that we might have to put some or all of the crew back on hibernation drugs again, so the eventual decision seemed pretty much inevitable.

***Mars tek** [13] - food, glorious food...*

What do you do to make life better for people who are having a hard time and expect to continue that way for some time to come - and your options don't include salary increases or company cars or penthouse suites? Well, one way is to make the food better. Sounds silly, huh? Not at all, good food, i.e., food that is tasty and interesting as well as nutritious, is an important part of the quality of life. The old sci-fi idea of reducing meals to pills popped when necessary is wildly unrealistic, psychologically as well as physically (digestible food has a minimum bulk that would be totally infeasible to reduce to pills, something that should be obvious from a few moments reflection). When life is tough and R&R time and opportunities are limited, good food in the company of family, friends and workmates becomes key to survival.

So, far from having a mundane and Spartan diet calculated to provide the maximum nutrition in the minimum time, Mars probably has a higher concentration of amateur gourmets than any group of people in the solar system outside of catering colleges. Growing interesting plants and cooking them in interesting ways, along with the limited supply of traditional farm animals and their products (sorry, Mars isn't all-vegetarian), together with the far less limited supply of bacteria, fungus and algae based foods - from booze through truffles to soy sauce and onwards to ever more adventurous culinary experiments -

*became, if not a global obsession (the Mars globe, that is),
certainly a pretty conspicuous feature of Mars life. Access to
extreme sports or haute couture might be somewhat limited, but
the average Martian eats better than any but the richest and most
discerning Earth gourmets.*

Tom and Jerry

Unfortunately the medical emergency gave some nutter high in
Earth space admin an opportunity to air his brilliant idea: do the
same with the Hope as with Rescuer, i.e. accelerate again to a
higher speed and use Mars atmosphere to brake at the other end. I
couldn't believe I was hearing this. I genuinely believed it was a
joke when it was first suggested to me. I mean, we're talking about
a vessel kliks across and weighing tens of thousands of tons at
Earth normal gravity (despite being made of foam) and carrying
several hundred people, not all of whom were as tough as your
average astronaut (including several babies born en-route, despite
everyone supposedly being on contraceptives). I did my damnedest
to suppress the idea, it was definitely up there in the top ten world's
worst ideas in history, but it was inevitable it would soon be leaked
to the media (space security these days making the average
colander look pretty watertight), at which point it would take on a
life all of its own. I wasn't aware that things had been flagging,
media-wise, but after the furore that greeted this announcement
(or, rather, leaked whisper), they certainly seemed to have been. I
quickly realised that in the gung-ho atmosphere generated by the
(largely) successful re-supply I'd look a pretty mean spirit to pour
cold water on this latest wonder without some pretty good
technical backup; so I gritted my teeth and waited for the sim
results.

They actually came out not as bad as I'd hoped; which, from a realistic standpoint, means pretty disastrous. I was miffed, I'd counted on the sims to show what a truly terrible idea it was and they'd shown instead that it wasn't an impossibly bad one. Notice, I didn't say 'good', the sims showed it was a risky long-shot rather than an easy-peasy ride, but when you have the world's media mincing reality all around you, trying to get a sane word in edgeways is one of life's harder and more futile jobs. I spent what seemed like half of eternity closeted in 'secret' meetings (excuse the quotes, ref my previous comment on security) but was only actually a week, before deciding on a cut-down version I'd suggested (well, shouted and screamed would be more accurate), one that would only waste a lot of fuel (that we'd almost certainly need later) and restricted the risks to a couple of our best people and a load of essential equipment and supplies...

It would get additional help to the Chinese vessel two weeks earlier, which, fair enough, might prove critical if anything else went wrong for them - but, in private, I still counted it as a supremely silly idea that we'd probably sincerely regret later. I'd done my best and minimised the risk as far as possible, enabling us to connect up with the Chinese without braking the Hope more than originally planned (which was at the safety limit in the first place). The plan was to indeed use another version of the Rescuer approach, only this time with a cargo pod with sufficient reinforcement to take the heavy g loads. It was only feasible because of the sheer quantity of engineering expertise and materials on the Hope. We attached two reconnaissance shuttles to the reinforced pod, with extra fuel in the shuttles replacing their usual crew complement, with two of the hardiest and most experienced astronauts in the pod, who would be encased in wads of protective foam and heavy-duty spacesuits during high-g periods, along with the most vital supplies.

The pod would be heavily accelerated in several bursts up to the halfway point between our current position and the Chinese vessel, then reversed and decelerated the same way, arriving, hopefully, at a standstill alongside it, while we - by now a week behind the pod - would continue on past in a week's time and take another week to get into a sensible orbit around Mars and then also be within shouting distance of the Chinese. I don't know if it saved any lives (it made no difference to the comatose Chinese astronaut, they had to pull the plug on him anyway), but it sure as hell put the sparkle back into the media's collective eyes... Nevertheless it cost us a lot of fuel and engineering time, two things perennially in short supply in ventures of this magnitude, so I wasn't best pleased with the dildo who'd forced it on us. Ah well.

The two astronauts who were to go in the pod were Thomas Brand and Gerald Asimo, alias - inevitably - Tom and Jerry (a cat and mouse from a mid-twentieth century animation, frequently revived), a further boon to the Earth's media, who, in my opinion, were getting more than their fair share of lucky breaks (though not so lucky for those at the sharp end). Mind you, no one in their right mind would make anything of this within their physical presence, they were both martial arts black belts and built like brick shit-houses; but the media presenters were a long way away. Tom and Jerry were ecstatic at what they saw as a 'real fun mission', typical astronauts I suppose, but I was pretty pissed at sending arguably the two best people out of the whole crew and had fought against it. Naturally I was overruled, and I couldn't deny their suitability for the job, not only were they individually well-qualified and capable but they worked together superbly, a valuable extra safety factor in the tricky situations that would undoubtedly arise during the pod mission.

These situations were highly likely as a by-product of the haste with which this sub-project had to be put together, compounded by the haste with which *everything* in the Hope's mission had had to be done. Normally, the planning for complex, long-distance missions lasts for years and involves hundreds, if not thousands, of individuals, and tens of thousands of sims and physical safety checks: we hadn't had the time for more than a tiny fraction of this. We were lucky in having the best space sims that had ever existed and also in having a disproportionate number of very competent people to hand on the Hope - but we knew we were pushing our luck all the same. The pod was a pretty ungainly vehicle, two hundred metres long and fifty square in cross-section, and, obviously, wasn't designed for independent flight, especially high acceleration / deceleration. We gave it a copy of the Hope's SAI, now updated with the detailed design plans and experience of the Chinese vessel beamed back by Rescuer, but we knew we'd be heavily dependent on Tom and Jerry's navigational and manoeuvring skills, and quite possibly their space fabrication skills as well if things came adrift on the pod, a very likely eventuality.

In the end things went much more smoothly than we had any right to expect - but then a little good luck was long overdue on Mars missions. Even so, Tom and Jerry were kept busy nearly every moment they weren't actually strapped down in the anti-g cocoons, and used just about every tool we kitted them out with - a number of the added struts and panels failed or got close to failure due to the (for the pod) extreme stresses. At one point they even had to do running repairs on one of the shuttle engines, a difficult feat even in normal conditions (that is, if space can ever have a word like 'normal' applied to it, which is debatable). We also lost contact just before they were due in the vicinity of the Chinese vessel, which gave us all the jitters for half a day. So when we eventually got back in contact and found they'd made it with both themselves and the vehicle more or less intact - if severely strained - we cheered more with relief than gladness at the success of this third mission.

The Chinese weren't in fact in very good shape when Tom and

Jerry arrived, with almost every crew member exhausted, sick and half-starved. But alive; and once the extra oxygen, water, food and drugs were distributed they had a two-thirds complement in a passably fit state within three days, a tribute to their inordinate toughness (and, it has to be said, to the care in their selection by the Chinese government).

7 PHOBOS

Mars tek *[14] - wherefore the commons...*

On Mars secure space is at a premium. Note that word 'secure': there's plenty of space on the surface - it just lacks a few necessities, like breathable air and protection from cosmic and solar radiation. Therefore living accommodation is a little more Spartan and a lot more communal than Earth average. The idea (the Earth idea, that is) was to start off this way and gradually relax into more Earth-like living conditions. Fortunately none of the early settlers shared this illusion - everyone who stepped out onto the Martian surface for the first time knew immediately that here was a place where humankind must work together and share and share alike. Or die. So a more communal life, where both facilities and responsibilities are shared by everyone, became the norm from the start. Naturally this was viewed with alarm by many Earth governments, but the extreme distance, combined with the early media exposure of life on Mars, protected the Martians from early military action, after which the situation became a fait accompli.

So Martian architecture had radically different requirements to satisfy from those on Earth, in particular the distinction between private and public space was far less sharp on Mars. The need for privacy, a fairly elastic psychological characteristic that varies immensely between cultures, was not absent on Mars - far from it, Martians are stubbornly independent by and large, and in such a hostile environment the ability to think for yourself is essential, so Martians are no hive-like society without individuality. Nevertheless, the tunnels and caves, which rapidly grew into warrens and caverns, were built for efficient provision of living space and associated services, including recycling, rather than the creation of desirable properties. It was the customs and agreements, enforced by common action rather than the police force or militia, which made allowance for those who wished not to be disturbed to not be so. Quiet study and work areas in M-GN-based libraries were given a high priority early on, though everyone also had a small amount of living and storage space protected by standard electronic locks.

Having a big house on the hill, though, or building large palaces or temples to your God/s, became quaint Earth history, with no place on a world whose people were confident and outward-looking even in the earliest birth-throes of their new society, and which, to confound those who predicted a steady deterioration of capability of a culture with so few apparent resources, would eventually become the major source of human seed for the stars.

Arrival

We were now ready for the first stage of our combined operation. The Chinese government had dispatched additional envoys and advisor's to join the world space administration and had proved more amenable to creating sensible joint objectives than I'd dared hope. The first one of these was to establish a base station on Phobos, the bigger of Mars two tiny moons, on which we'd get our joint act together, bringing everyone up to a good standard of fitness (not just the Chinese crew, everyone needed a boost from new activity and some leg-stretching after the long journey), and building a solid solar-energy-powered station with significant food production and foam manufacturing capacity. We weren't going to set foot on Mars itself until we were good and ready, despite the howls of the media (who were just being greedy, anyway, as there would be no shortage of gob-smacking footage from the Phobos base).

We established Phobos base on the Mars side, so shielding ourselves from the sun while doing the building work; this was an important consideration after such a tiring journey, radiation is more damaging when you're DNA repair systems aren't fully up to scratch (though some found it a bit vertiginous at first to have Mars filling most of the sky above their heads). Having a base on Phobos gave us a number of advantages: for starters it would enable us to finish engineering some of the systems we hadn't had time to complete on the journey, including a robust space / Mars surface transport system; it gave everyone time to come to full fitness before the rigours of Mars - one of the first things we did was build a bigger gravity wheel than we could manage on the Hope, to get everyone's cardiovascular and skeletomuscular systems back up to full strength after the weakening low gravity of the trip; it enabled us to build up stocks of energy, food and materials (Phobos was a carbonaceous asteroid in origin - in other words there were plenty of carbon-based compounds around to convert into food and fuel); and it gave us time to draw breath and do some hard strategic thinking about how to crack a problem that had defeated all expeditions so far - how to successfully colonise Mars itself.

One of the things we'd saved space and fuel on by not carrying it from Earth was the heavy-duty foam we were going to need to get the majority of the equipment - the (for us) heavy stuff - down to Mars. Essentially we were going to create a number of massive footballs with thick, elastic foam walls, trailing drag lines to slow them down reasonably quickly (else they might bounce for dozens of kliks and end up all over the place). The sensitive stuff - like people - would be using massive combined foam bloop / rocket landers that used carbon dioxide as ion fuel (generated on Phobos or garnered from the edge of the Martian atmosphere), energised by power cells charged by the ultra-high-efficiency solar cells littered over the sunny side of Phobos. We were taking the approach right from the start of using local materials wherever we could, even if it meant taking a little longer to get going (and ultimately we'd have no choice in the matter, we either used local materials or went home).

Phobos station was OK for food more or less indefinitely as soon as the greenhouses were fully operational, and it was even a reasonably varied diet, if a little light on animal protein (mostly substituted by algae at this stage anyway). It was also doing well on the energy front, as already noted, and producing almost any amount of rock and CHON based foam. There was a (temporary) shortage of metals, and of some esoteric hydrocarbons (basically we didn't want to build the more extensive chemical converters and separators until we made landfall), and nitrogen was in fairly short supply, but there was just about enough to get by of everything for this period before landing on Mars proper. The media were soon baying for a Mars landing, but luckily both mission commanders were tough nuts who could smile nicely and tell the media and their masters to take a hike - politely of course... (command was jointly held between the Hope's and Chinese captains - something I had had to fight tooth and nail for, as I was sure that humbling the Chinese by making their captain subordinate to the Hopes was more of a recipe for trouble than the difficulties of shared command).

This breather on Phobos was essential; we had to get our collective act together and start doing things in a measured way instead of in constant haste. So everyone got the chance of some R&R while a robust station was built on Phobos with all essential systems in good order and a reasonable level of manufacturing capacity constructed. We didn't entirely dismantle Phobos - we wanted a stable base for a space station in Mars orbit anyway - but we took quite a bite out of it. We made sure, though, to keep the total mass of the station plus Hope plus the Chinese vessel plus Phobos reasonably constant, to ensure no destabilisation of its orbit. This period gave the planners, both my team on Earth and the Mars team on Phobos, time to do a proper job of putting together the next critical steps in Mars colonisation (the views of the colonisers themselves were input through electronic referenda). Altogether we spent two years on Phobos before going down. It might sound like a long delay but we had a lot to do and the time went fast.

8 MARS

Mars tek *[15] - on the road...*

Long before we attempt (if we do) to terraform Mars, or just build a better atmosphere / climate, or whatever, we'll need to make a number of more mundane (and achievable) changes to the Martian surface. In particular, we'll need to make it a safer place for travellers. Just as in the more inhospitable but inhabited places on Earth, like the high Alps or Siberia, we'll need to build the equivalent of way-stop cabins where weary travellers can shut the door on the elements and get a fire going to cook a bite to eat before collapsing on some makeshift bunks to recover from their hellish journey through hostile terrain and bad weather. The Mars equivalent would be a fairly deep hole in the ground (more than three meters, though with a bank of solar panels on the surface) with an accessible though well-protected and sealed air-lock (a difficult combination) and a hot-rock heater rather than a log fire - though the bunk beds might look a little similar... Such way stations represent, automation notwithstanding, a heavy commitment of work and resources, so they probably wouldn't happen in the initial establishment phase, when every second and gram of material is precious, but in the secondary phase after a couple of years of building main bases.

As well as reasonably frequent way stations (no more than three reasonably fast journey days apart, perhaps) there would need to be secondary bases (e.g. at polar ice collection points) which, though not permanently occupied, would have more extensive facilities such as vehicle refuelling and repair and M-GN repeaters, as well as spare vehicles of more rudimentary design (such as the 'Marcycles'). Such bases would act as refuelling stops and would have their own power generation, probably both solar and hot-rock, and associated fuel production for both fuel cells and hydrocarbon engines. They would also be enablers for the scientific work, including detailed cartographic and geomagnetic mapping, that would need to start as soon as bare survival was assured.

Completing a reasonably comprehensive network of way stations and secondary bases would signal the end of initial colonisation - being no more than a few days away from a place of refuge anywhere you go is always a sign of the development of civilisation: Martians would then start looking at the sky and thinking about the next interesting place...

Landfall

Both the military types (a few had been sneaked in amongst us...) and the media were baying for an invasion-like armada to sweep down to the Martian surface from Phobos. The majority of sensible people, however, including both captains, firmly rejected such a silly idea, so we put together a comprehensive landing plan - not that the media would be deprived of their spectacle, it just wouldn't happen all at once. A phased landing, with the footballs sent ahead followed by an initial task force to prepare for the bulk of later arrivals, made a lot more sense - for starters the chances of vehicles running into one another would be minimised rather than maximised as in the armada approach.

Even so it was still incredibly impressive, and fully captured by the usual flotilla of remotes and drones, designed to gladden the hearts of media people everywhere. Several dozen footballs were carefully released into minimum-energy glide (or, rather, dropping brick) paths, designed to keep them within a reasonable search area while minimising the chances of bumping into one another (something which could actually do more damage than hitting solid rock, believe it or not). The injection technique was to carry the footballs one at a time on a large shuttle that slowed to just above stalling at a fairly low height, imparting a forward turning force to each football just as it was released so it would hit the ground spinning fast enough to even out the damaging impact forces over as much of the ball's resilient foam skin as possible without speeding it up too much on the ground - a tricky balance. Once released it was tracked by the aforementioned remotes / drones (at least they had some useful purpose...) and every bump, bounce and crunch lovingly recorded for the delectation of Earth (by now the proportion of Earth's population addicted to Martian soaps derived from our footage approached 100%).

Landing the people was to be a more sedate affair, using very low mass shuttle-like planes that had just enough fuel to land but were robust enough to be re-usable (hopefully...) once they were refitted for the electric sled to be built on Olympus Mons for space injection (Olympus Mons was 25 kliks high, with significantly lower gravity and virtually no atmosphere at all at the top - made to be a spaceship launcher really). The shuttles were encased in the usual voluminous hi-impact, ultra low-weight foam, which would also act as temporary radiation buffers and enable the shuttles to provide safe accommodation while the subsurface shelters were built. Controlling them wasn't as precise as the big ships but was good enough to select sensible landing sites and not run into one another. The idea was to get everyone within comfortable surface travelling time of both each other and the footballs, though most of the latter would still have to be moved quite some distance.

The footballs were dropped one every hour or so for several days, with results of earlier drops fed back to redirect flight paths and drop points of later ones. Overall we didn't do too badly, with about ten percent damaged but repairable and only two spectacularly destroyed (an acceptable loss compared with the value of the media footage - the Chinese captain remarked afterwards that if it had all gone perfectly we'd have had to send down a couple more full of bright junk and programmed to fall over cliffs etc...).

The shuttles were a different matter, we had absolutely *no* intention of providing Earth media with footage of our people being mashed in crash landings, however great the soap value... The shuttles not only had their foam overcoats but were fairly well armoured, and everyone descended wearing their surface suits despite being cushioned in foam webbing into the bargain. Even if they did hit hard we intended everyone to walk away uninjured, as far as it was humanly possible to arrange. Obviously people with physical problems - and there were bound to be some, over such a long journey and relatively large number of people, who had injured themselves or been disabled by some condition or another (as well as the babies of course...) - had to be left on Phobos, along with a sufficiently strong crew to run everything. These last had been selected by the usual drawing of electronic short straws - though Tom and Jerry were exempted by universal agreement (despite their feeble protests at being singled out for special treatment). The two captains had tossed a coin as to who went down and who stayed on Phobos - the Chinese captain won (needless to say the winner went down to Mars surface).

As mentioned, the shuttles went in two groups, also singly at regular intervals, with the first group establishing communications and reporting back on ground conditions before the second descended. There were a few mishaps with subsequent hard landings, which again provided wonderfully entertaining footage - but not, thanks to our paranoid protection plans, extending to deaths or serious injuries (though we played up what minor injuries there were to keep the media people happy). The most spectacular of all was a shuttle that got its flight plan correct but was unlucky enough to hit a super-low-resistance surface consisting of a layer of sand-like grit (most Martian 'sand' is more like dust) spread fairly evenly over a hard, level rock surface. So instead of gently grinding to a halt over a mile or so it scooted twenty miles and ran smack into a couple of footballs. Luckily the team leader of the shuttle realised what was happening almost immediately and warned everyone to stay strapped in despite the relatively smooth ride, so when they cannoned into the footballs they were all fully protected. There were still a few minor injuries but the main casualty was the shuttle itself (remember the footballs were designed for this sort of thing), which was obviously destined to be one of the few *not* to be re-used. It also meant they were a fairly long way from the bulk of other shuttles and more or less had to be rescued by the other teams pooling people and equipment to collect them. Great footage, of course...

9 COLONY

Mars tek *[16] - is everybody happy?..*

Reading about life for the early Mars colonisers might give the impression it was all work and no play, survival being all. It can't be denied that early Mars colonisation was a pretty intense process with not a lot of room for error, but it would be wrong to think you can't have fun on Mars. Recreation - R & R - getting away from it all - chilling out - whatever, this is important stuff, and the harder you work the more important play becomes. The fact is that Mars has some solid recreational advantages. For starters, you can fly...

Well, sort of; Mars' gravity is only a third that of Earth, so if you inflate a large dome or dig a large cavern, even at half Earth-normal air pressure (about the maximum it's sensible to pressurise to on Mars) you can give people wings and they can fly (though we're talking about very fit people remember). Not for long, it still takes a lot of energy, and people still aren't designed like birds, but it's a feasible thing to do, engineering-wise, and given a colony of dare-devil tekies it was inevitable it was going to happen not long after the early emergency conditions had abated. Similarly, the only other common Mars vehicle, alongside the all-singing-and-dancing Rover, was a similar-looking contraption without the heavy-duty survival gear and made of super-lightweight foams. The Fido (presumably named by a dog-lover with a sense of humour) could also go anywhere, but, because it was so light, yet still strong enough to be seriously abused, it was faster and could do things a heavier vehicle couldn't; you could run it over cliffs (and almost up cliffs) and bounce it across large-rock fields and over out-gassing polar plains etcetera - anything you could take it could.

These and other pursuits, some quieter and some even zanier, enabled Martians to let their hair down when off-duty at last, and presage a future where Mars is as much an R&R resort as a serious staging post for humanity to prepare itself for the stars.

Start-up

Establishing a self-sustaining colony on a cold inhospitable rock with a low-pressure carbon dioxide atmosphere full of abrasive dust which frequently rouses itself into furious storms that block sunlight and make it virtually impossible to travel on the surface has its difficulties... To give you an idea of a typical Martian problem lets look at the effects of dust on gathering solar energy - the major long-term power source, assuming nuclear as a temporary option only. Despite the obscuring effects of dust storms there's still enough sunlight to go round - provided firstly that you can neutralise the dust's abrasiveness. This had already defeated earlier expeditions - whose remaining materials we would cannibalise in due course - but the tek for coating artefacts with diamond was now sufficiently advanced to use anywhere, including Mars, so we simply coated everything that would ever be exposed on the Martian surface with diamond film. Luckily this only reduced the efficiency of solar cells by a few percent, leaving plenty of usable energy for our purposes, though it meant we had to increase the area for solar collection even more, but this was no bad thing as we used the acres of collection area as roofs for greenhouses and exercise areas.

But that wasn't the end of the problems with dust for solar collection, there was also the difficulty of designing the roofs to resist other effects of the dust. The ideal would be flat roofs , which would collect energy for most of the day without needing to be moved to track the sun and would also offer least resistance to dust storms - but flat roofs would be rapidly obscured by a layer of dust. Having the roofs in the traditional inverted V, though efficient at minimising the effort needed to keep clear of dust, presented plenty of resistance to the frequent high winds, which, though considerably less powerful than those of Earth, still packed a punch and would entail substantial reinforcement. So we settled for roofs with a semi-circular cross-section, which were more difficult to manufacture and required higher-efficiency solar cells, which in turn were also more difficult to manufacture. But at least they were more easily kept free of dust (cleaner robots to traverse the roofs and blow dust off the top surface into the gutters, and a simple mechanism for sucking the dust out of the gutters).

This process of designing around Mars sheer orneriness was typical of all activities on Mars: shelter, transport, food production, mining, coms, recycling... Living on Mars wasn't a lot easier than living in space, truth be told. This should have been obvious right from the start, but apparently it wasn't. Perhaps the sci-fi fairy tales of earlier centuries had clouded our collective vision. Nevertheless, by this time the lesson had been learnt - the hard way, so we were under no illusions as to the beneficence of Mars: for 'Red Planet' read red for danger. So once down everyone set about grimly prepared for tough times ahead; first gathering the footballs so we had our major resources in one place. The next priority was to establish a well-protected base with a reliable power source, which would enable us to continue development under cover for a while. This initial base was inevitably a compromise between being close to a sensible place to land relatively fragile craft, the need for access to water-ice, reasonable levels of sunshine, and access to the means for energy-efficient injection into low orbit so we could travel to and from Phobos station, i.e. fairly close to Olympus Mons. Tricky.

Mars tek [17] - necessity is the mother...

On the face of it, tek is tek, and location - unlike housing - is immaterial. But of course, in the real world, nothing is so simple. In the early days all Mars R&D was necessarily derivative from Earth. Inevitably, though, Mars' concerns soon diverged from those of Earth. For example, though Earth development of closed systems was by now very advanced, mostly thanks to the demands of space science, it was quite inadequate for Mars colonists, whose initial huge efforts to build up stores of CHON, by transporting large quantities of water / carbon dioxide ice, and as by-products of rock processing, couldn't possibly continue without a very high level of CHON recycling if the colony was to grow to any reasonably self-sustaining size. So the Martian version of a closed-cycle system was radically more stringent than its Earth counterpart, and Martian systems became the gold standard for closed-cycle processing within a short time of the establishment of independent Martian R&D.

Similarly, for Earth the space effort was a luxury, arguably an important spiritual outlet for its energies, but not exactly essential to life (at least in the short term...). On Mars, contrariwise, space capability was not only the umbilical cord to Earth (albeit too long a cord to be of any real practical use) but also a major, if not the major, contributor to the Martian planetary info system, and a major source of manufactured goods (and, once several additional power sats had been established to utilise continuous sunlight, the major uninterrupted power supply of any magnitude). The direct contributions to daily life on Mars of space-based tek meant that its development soon outstripped that of Earth, despite the immensely greater resources available to earth tekkies. Another important area was energy efficiency, Mars had no energy to waste and had to use what it had optimally, so energy-efficient space transport had a doubly high priority.

Advanced R&D for closed-cycle systems, space tek and energy-efficient machines, together with developments in other areas relevant to life on Mars, inevitably caused Mars scitek to depart from that of Earth from very early on; initially in small ways, but soon in radical and interesting ways, supporting the view of visionaries centuries before who had believed that humankind would eventually have to expand its horizons beyond the Earth if it was to reach its full potential.

Colony

The best we could come up with was a base half-way between Olympus Mons and the Milankovitz crater. It was close enough to the northern ice cap to have valleys nearby that were sufficiently sheltered to have some water-ice at the bottom, and also was near the Vastitas Borealis, the huge plain in the Northwest quadrant, with several good landing sites nearby. We had a little extra luck (unlike just about everyone before us) in that the weather in the area stayed stable for several months - not that we hadn't tried to predict a stable period and launch accordingly, but Martian weather is generally as hard to predict as that of Earth's used to be, if rather less complex in character. This first surface base, compromise that it was, was only marginally viable as a full-blown population centre, we really needed one nearer the equator to make better use of the weaker sun on Mars. That would have to wait, however, until we'd established good transport and coms between Phobos and Mars surface. The intense solar energy collection on Phobos would enable them to provide most of the power to drive both ends of the link, though we had to build the rail on Olympus Mons in the first place.

In theory, we also had a heavy scientific exploration and analysis workload, but my agenda had this at a rather lower level than some other interested parties. I knew we'd get away with it if we provided the media with all the real 'live' space opera footage they could use... It's not that I had anything against Martian science development, just that I knew we wouldn't make it unless we concentrated very hard indeed on survival, consigning non-essentials not just to the back-burner while getting established but to oblivion. There were howls of protest but no-one could accuse the Martian colonists of lazing around, the media footage showed the stark reality of establishing a foothold on a tough world in wincing detail. We had to have time before inessentials got a look in and that was that.

Even so it wasn't all hair shirts, human beings have a way of enjoying themselves however hard their circumstances, and building a new world is exhilarating and fun as well as hard work. As soon as we'd built the basics of Olympus Station (as it was half-way between Olympus Mons and Milankovich Crater I suppose it should have been Olympus-Milankovich Station, but that was too much of a mouthful - and the Greek mythology buffs went for 'Olympus' in a big way for obvious reasons) it was party-time - at least in the few moments spare from all that constructing of life-support infrastructure.

Once we'd got the base and a workable shuttle link with Phobos, where carbon dioxide and water ice could be converted to useful fuel and materials, life could settle into some sort of order (the word 'normal' hardly applied at this stage or for some time to come). This took another year and a half, by which time we knew we'd basically cracked it - especially as almost nobody was interested in returning to Earth, though plenty wanted their kith and kin and friends to join them. In fact there was increasing clamour to open up a regular colonist route to Mars, despite the - by now well-televised - rigours of the journey. I resisted this for the initial period of establishment as I knew the addition of more colonists this early would over-stretch the facilities they'd so painfully constructed, but it was inevitable in the longer run (and, anyway, *I* wanted to go as well). The selection process was tough, the cost was high, the facilities were sparse, and no-one (well, almost no-one...) got an easy ride; yet there was never a shortage of qualified takers.

I had other agendas, not only did I not believe that Mars was necessarily the best bet in the long term for the conquest of space (it was too hard to accumulate the spare resources required for its inhabitants to go much further any time soon) but I already had other ventures - foam-based of course - planned and in XR development (the asteroids and Venus, for starters). These, together with my continuing role as Mars spokesperson / planner, seemed to always stop me from quite being able to take the trip to the red planet myself. But I'll get there some day.

Glossary

PA   Personal Assistant: here, a disembodied SAI tailored for a particular person

SAI   Strong Artificial Intelligence – a human level AI

GN   Global Net: future version of the internet

supersim   a simulation very close to physical reality

FW   the Foam World XR supersim

CHON   Carbon, Hydrogen, Oxygen and Nitrogen

XR   future version of Virtual Reality plus Augmented Reality

M-GN   GN for Mars

www.ingramcontent.com/pod-product-compliance
Lightning Source LLC
Chambersburg PA
CBHW060650260626
47161CB00008B/3077